Stories To Take To Your Grave

Wandering Souls

Undertaker Books

UNDERTAKER BOOKS
www.undertakerbooks.com

Contents

INTRODUCTION

Sometimes writing anthology introductions is easy.

Sometimes I pawn them off on someone else (Hi Avery!).

Other times I sit staring at a blank document, wondering what I should write.

I mean, it feels kind of pompous as an editor to sit here and tell you this is a kick-ass anthology. Don't get me wrong—it is a kick-ass anthology, but it feels arrogant to say so. But someone has to say it.

THIS IS A KICK-ASS ANTHOLOGY.

Some of my favorite stories are included in these pages. That may seem kind of obvious to you, dear reader, because I picked them to be part of this anthology. But there's not a story here that I regret including, and I'd recommend them all in a heartbeat.

At it's core, Wandering Souls is an anthology of ghost stories. But it's also so much more than that. Each story brings something different to the table, a different perspective of life beyond the veil. And yet, each story is at it's essence human, something that you can relate to as a reader and enjoy in spite of (or because of) the horrors in the story.

It was a lot of fun to put together, and I hope you enjoy reading it.

D.L. Winchester
January 3, 2025
Newport, TN

STORIES TO TAKE TO YOUR GRAVE

WANDERING SOULS EDITION

You'll Be All over the Papers

Keller Agre

G *reat-great-great-grandfather is rolling in his grave.*
He'd be ashamed of how one of his own lived.

My tired seventeen-year-old sedan trudged down the road on its last leg. The waving marsh grass on either side beckoned me to the once world-famous Crane Island. My family had visited this barrier island off the coast of Georgia often in the late 19th century. As I traveled the streets, I could almost hear the faint echoes of hooves on cobblestones as I imagined horse-drawn carriages transporting the world's influential men from beach to hunting grounds.

My relative who first stepped foot onto Crane Island's natural beaches was George Wright, newspaper tycoon. Would he cringe seeing the island today so accessible and peopled by the shorts-wearing middle and lower classes? I hated to admit I fell into this demographic. Our family's lifestyle had been modest since George sold his newspaper, *The Maine Gazette*, to what is now *The Canal Street Journal* in the late 1800s. For some unknown reason, our family received almost none of the money after he died. George got in a few good years elbow-rubbing with some of history's most powerful men before succumbing to heart disease, something he kept secret until the end, inside the Crane Island Club Resort. This resort, also my destination, served as a getaway for wealthy men and their families during the winter months.

I passed the ruins of the Henderson house. I recognized it from old photographs I looked at often. The Alexander cottage seemed hollow and abandoned compared to the sepia image burned into my mind from family photo albums. The boats parked in the marina were small compared to what George would use to ferry to the island.

After years of working my monotonous accounting job, I needed some time away. I saved up for a relaxing weekend by myself, hoping to have some fun living like my ancestor had for a short time. Growing up, I certainly told enough people about my heritage, which sparked questions such as, "Why aren't you rich now?" My response was always an embarrassing lie about our preference for simplicity and moderation.

As I pulled into the club's grounds, I was greeted by a vintage Ford Model-T and a pair of gentlemen, clad all in white, playing croquet. I rolled my window down to get an unfiltered view of the club along with its sounds and smells. The scent of freshly cut grass mingled with the salty breeze. Gulls sounded their high, piercing call from rustling palm trees, providing a stark contrast to the urban landscape I had grown accustomed to in midtown Atlanta. The club itself was an ornate tan building with a turret that reminded me of a sandcastle. After parking in the adjacent lot, I approached the vintage car. The black doors, waxed to shine, reflected the club in a distorted image. I imagined myself sitting in the driver's seat, taking in all the looks from jealous faces. I lugged my suitcase as quickly as I could toward the front desk.

"Hello, sir, and welcome to the Crane Island Club Resort," the teenager said with little effort. His wrinkled slacks and basketball shoes told me he didn't take this gig seriously. I couldn't understand why such a high-end resort entrusted him with the front desk when an older man, whom I assumed to be his supervisor, emerged from behind a door marked "Employees Only" in gold lettering.

"Hi. Checking in," I said.

"What's the name?" the teenager asked.

"Henry Wright."

He looked up from the tablet.

"Wright?" he asked.

"Yes," I said, standing up a little straighter.

"You'll be in the...Wright suite. Room 3315."

"The Wright suite? Like George Wright?"

"Yes, sir. Are you related to him, by chance?"

"I am," I said. "But I thought I booked a different room."

He perked up and said, "You did. We upgraded you free of charge to one of our best suites."

I smiled. "What makes it one of your best?"

The teenager glanced at his superior as if waiting for him to answer. When the older man offered no help, the kid turned back and gave me his best customer service smile.

"The room is spacious and beautifully decorated, complete with a large balcony. Only a few rooms have that. It also comes with a chance to experience some...unique phenomena. Do you read the paper by chance?"

"No," I laughed. "Unless it's on my phone."

The teen laughed politely and said, "Well, George Wright would ask for a copy of *The Canal Street Journal* and coffee every morning. We've had guests tell us when they've ordered a newspaper and coffee to the Wright Suite and then leave for a short time, they'll find the coffee drunk, and the newspaper disturbed as if someone has read it."

"Interesting," I said, breaking eye contact.

"Very," the teen replied. "We ask all guests who stay in that room if they'd like a newspaper delivered in the morning."

"Sure," I smiled. "Can you deliver coffee too?"

"Unfortunately, no," he said. "But there is a coffee machine in the room."

"Great. Thanks..." I checked the kid's name tag. "Jake."

"You're welcome. Enjoy your stay, Mr. Wright!"

I nodded and moved toward the nearby elevator. After a quick ride up to the third floor, the doors slid open, revealing a narrow hallway decorated with a patterned blue and white rug. I pictured myself walking down this hall back then, tipping my hat to beautiful young women as they passed by. I used the key card to unlock my room, breaking the historical fantasy for a moment, and entered.

The room was modest compared to the modern luxury hotels I'd been in. Each piece of furniture was made from dark wood. Red fabrics with flower patterns adorned the seats and bed. In the corner sat an antique desk. I hoped, but doubted, this was the same desk George used. The room's smell, a mix of flowers and lemon-scented cleaning spray, reminded me of my grandparents' living room. There was an alcove at one end which housed a dining room table. The paint that covered the crown molding was chipping in places, reminding me of my apartment back home. A white door led to a balcony that overlooked the Atlantic Ocean. The only thing I disliked was a small TV sitting on top of the dresser, which felt out of place.

After unpacking, I grabbed a book and sat on the balcony to read. I took in the salty air and surveyed the courtyard below, where people putzed around, pointing their fingers and cell phone cameras at the hotel. I guessed they were not staying at the resort and came only to view the extravagant building. Maybe they would see me sitting in a white rocking chair, somewhat handsome and well dressed, and think I was well off.

A few hours passed, and I came back inside hungry. I called the front desk and arranged for an early dinner at their sister resort, the less historic and pricey Crane Island Ocean Club, and a shuttle to take me to and from.

I removed the only suit I owned from the closet and laid it out on the bed.

A chill traveled up my spine.

I shuddered and closed my eyes. Icy air traveled into my lungs like chilled tea hitting a warm stomach. I opened my eyes.

A man stood on the other side of the bed. A butler.

A gold watch chain hung from the vest of his dark suit. He held a leather bag in front of him with both hands. His large mustache and oily black hair were both out of place and yet appropriate within the room's decor.

"Would you like that suit pressed, Mr. Wright?" he asked.

I didn't respond. I jumped from thought to thought, trying to make sense of who or what was in front of me. The door remained locked.

"No, thank you...sir," I responded.

"Very well," he said. "And will Mrs. Wright be joining you this evening?"

"No," I said.

"Excellent," the butler smiled. "Then I shall prepare the bathroom for tonight's activities."

"Activities?" I asked. "I don't know what you mean."

"Of course, sir, very good." The butler winked. "I'm pleased to see you harbor no ill will against me after what happened. You must know, I did it to protect the both of us."

"After *what* happened?" I asked.

He vanished. The room's temperature returned to normal.

What activities was he talking about? Mrs. Wright? He must've mistaken me for George.

I smiled at this idea. I always knew spirits existed. Another thing I was right about. The ghosts were welcoming me to the place where I belong. I hoped George would show up next.

The rotary phone on the nightstand rang, and I picked up the receiver.

"Hello?"

"Your shuttle is here, Mr. Wright," a male voice said.

"Thank you. I'll be down in a sec," I said.

I rushed to throw on my suit, skipping the tie, and headed downstairs. The white van sat outside with a few others waiting in the back seat. I entered and took a spot in the front. No one dressed as well as I did. The couple in back chatted, without consideration of others, for the duration of the short ride to the sister resort.

"I had no idea there was so much history here. Anything else interesting about the resort I should know, honey?" the man said to the woman. His Midwestern accent both annoyed me and made me feel bad for them.

"There may or may not have been some murders," the woman said. I stopped tuning them out but didn't turn my head.

"What?" the man said. "Why didn't you lead with that? That's the most interesting thing you've told me."

"It was never proven. But who's to say it wasn't covered up? A lot of powerful men stayed here."

"Well, c'mon, share some details," the man asked.

"They found a girl washed up on the beach. She had fifty stab wounds all over her body."

"My goodness," the man gasped, causing me to roll my eyes. "And they didn't think it was a murder with fifty stab wounds?"

"Like I said, powerful men."

"Unbelievable," he said. "I mean, *duh*. She was obviously murdered. Didn't those people know *anything?*"

I gripped the seatbelt tight.

If only they had access to your genius during the investigation.

"I know," the woman said. "There's also an urban legend about it. The resort's drains flowed into the ocean back then. The morning after the girl's death, , the sea was red with blood. They say some mornings you can see the red water from the pier."

The man laughed. "Let's wake up early tomorrow and check."

"We would've been like everyone else. Eating it up. Apparently, the press coverage of the supposed murders sold out newspapers."

"I'd think so," the man said.

The couple's conversation continued and turned as boring as their grocery list. We arrived at the resort, and I exited the van in a hurry to avoid any unintended interaction. The host sat me at a table in the corner, as I'd requested, and I scanned the room. I couldn't believe how some of these people dressed. T-shirts and shorts and, most inappropriate, flip-flops. Who allowed them to dine in such an upscale restaurant? Didn't they have any respect for it or, at least, themselves? I tried to focus on myself. There was no point in getting worked up over other people, especially not *these* other people.

I ate my steak and enjoyed a few cocktails, making sure to order a respectable but not too pricey bourbon, before catching a ride back on the same shuttle.

I wanted to continue drinking.

The only bar in the entire resort was an eight-seat semi-circle in the main lobby. The rest of the lobby resembled an old hunting club. Mounted high on the walls, the heads of deer and boars observed, watching over the dimly lit space embellished with plush, dark leather chairs and mahogany tables. Fake plants sat atop the electric fireplaces. An unused chess board lingered in the corner. At this late hour, it was just me and the bartender. He sported a turn-of-the-century costume. His tall club collar under his pinstripe suit looked uncomfortable, but I appreciated the sentiment. I perused the drink menu and found drinks from different eras of the club's operation, going back as far as the

1880s. I ordered a "Hemingway Daiquiri" from the "Roaring Twenties" section of the list. I couldn't help but be transported back in time. After examining every bottle on the shelves, I asked the bartender: "Excuse me. Have you heard any reports of ghosts at the resort?"

"Plenty," the bartender said. "People love to say they saw someone walking along the balconies in a white suit at night. They're never able to provide any specific details."

"Interesting," I said. "Have you seen any?"

"I've had one encounter," he said, lifting an eyebrow.

"Can you tell me about it?" I asked.

"Of course, sir. But only because there's no one else around," he said and winked. "One night, we had a particularly lively evening at the bar. I think they were having a wedding on the grounds the next day. Anyway, I was cleaning up the glasses and heard a voice from behind me. It asked, 'Barkeep? Can I take a drink with me?' I turned around and there was a beautiful woman standing there in a gorgeous red dress. She looked straight out of the early aughts. Big hat with flowers on top, a sun umbrella, the whole thing. I didn't think much of it. People come here and pretend they're old money all the time."

I took a sip of my drink.

"I said, 'Of course, ma'am. What'll it be?' She said, 'As long as it's got whiskey, I'm a happy girl.' I made her a drink, an old-fashioned, and asked, 'Would you like to charge it to the room?' She said, 'Yes. Only, I'm not sure which room that would be.' I asked, 'Why's that?' She said, 'I'm a guest of Mr. Wright.'"

I gripped my drink tighter.

The bartender continued, "She said, 'He's invited me here. Something about a job at the newspaper.' I didn't know what to say. I knew who Mr. Wright was. Part of the job requirement is knowing the club's history. I thought I'd just play along. I said, 'I'll take care of it. What's your name, miss?' She said her name was Florence. Florence Gibson. She thanked me for the drink and just as she reached for it...she disappeared." The bartender punctuated this last detail with a wave of his hand and wide eyes.

I stared at the man, waiting for him to continue.

"I thought it was weird, you know? So, I looked up this Florence Gibson. And guess what I find? She was murdered! They found her body washed up on a beach not far from here. I saw it in an article in *The Maine Gazette*, some newspaper that isn't around anymore. Isn't that strange?"

"Very," I said. "Quite a story."

"But here's where it gets even stranger. One day I was cleaning up the Wright suite after a guest checked out. A lot of the staff help with other jobs during the busy season. Anyway, I go into the bathroom, right? The whole room is ice cold. And then, I'm bending down to clean the shower when suddenly, I hear: 'Help me!' right in my ear! I looked and there was no one around. The bathroom was completely empty. Can you believe it?"

"No," I said. I finished my drink with one gulp and pushed the empty glass away.

"It's true. They never found out who killed that girl. But you know what I think?"

"It was George Wright?" I asked.

The bartender shrugged. "I wouldn't be surprised. Most of the men back then had dark secrets."

"You don't know what you're talking about!" I yelled, drawing stares from the few people that had joined us in the lobby.

"I'm sorry," I said quickly. "I think I've had one too many drinks. I need to head back to my room. Can I have the check?"

The bartender nodded and, after taking a few drink orders from newly arrived patrons who didn't know how to wait their turn, handed me the bill.

"Just write your room number and name and it'll be charged to your room."

I hesitated. Should I write my name down after the story? Wright was a common enough last name. I scribbled the information he requested, left a generous cash tip, and got up from the backless barstool. He picked up the paper, and as I moved toward the door. I felt his gaze on my back.

I barreled through the door and didn't look back. The hardwood stairs creaked with each step I took up to the third floor. The hallway's décor, less charming now, rushed by as I moved toward my room. My desire to see George's ghost had waned. After scanning my card, I gripped the door handle.

Ice cold.

I stood frozen in place. A chill crept up my arm and turned my spine to ice. Someone down the hall opened their door, knocking me out of my stupor. I entered the Wright suite.

Everything was as I had left it, and the temperature in the room was normal. I walked around the bed, checking in every direction. Nothing. I stared at the dark bathroom doorway.

Why am I so scared? Ghosts can't hurt you.

I charged, as if taking the offensive, into the bathroom and flipped on the lights. Still nothing. I turned to the shower.

He couldn't have killed her. George was a fine man.

I opened the heavy glass door and walked in. The air inside the shower carried the faint scent of soap. There was a small chip in the tile near the floor, below the shower head. I lowered myself and reached for it, feeling the cool, glossy surface beneath my fingertips.

The shower door slammed.

The walls reverberated, deafening me for a moment. I stood up and tried to open the door. It wouldn't budge. The air turned frigid. I could see my breath with each smoky exhale. My skin prickled.

What is going on? There's no lock on this thing.

A man walked into the bathroom.

He wore similar attire to the butler, only his suit was white, and he had no facial hair. He held a large hunting knife in his right hand.

"Good evening," he said.

I stood back up.

"Who are you?" I asked.

"Just a newspaper man trying to sell more copies. Who you are is much more important," he said, opening his palms to me.

"What're you talking about?" I asked.

"You'll be all over the papers," he said. "Isn't that marvelous? Although, I will say, it's usually a woman in your place."

I recognized him from old pictures. "George Wright? I'm your distant relative. Henry Wright."

"*You?*" he said, scrutinizing me from head to toe. "You're lying. No relative of mine would wear a suit so cheap. And look at your face. Have you shaved today?"

"It's been a long time since you sold the newspaper," I said. "None of the money made its way to me."

"I never should've sold *The Gazette*." George shook his head. "But I had no other option."

"Because you were sick?" I asked.

"Not exactly," he replied.

"Then why did you?" I asked.

"I should shut my pan. But there's a connection between us. Henry, was it? Typically, all I can do is rustle a paper or spill some coffee. It's been a long time since I've been able to appear like this."

A smile spread across my face. The great George Wright was right in front of me, accepting me as one of his own. He was everything I had imagined. If only I could've reached out and shook his hand. I wanted him to be real. For us to spend time together and have other people see us.

"I know you can keep a secret," he said. "And maybe you can learn a thing or two about how to get to the top. Our family needs to flourish, Henry."

I wished I had a pen and paper.

"It started small, of course. A fire. A mugging. But then I realized the great bottom fact of what *really* sold copies."

Florence Gibson.

"You killed?"

"That's right, Henry. I did it right where you're standing. Then I'd wash the blood down the drain and my butler would do the rest."

Shall I prepare the bathroom for tonight's activities? The ocean would be red with blood.

"The headlines outsold every other newspaper on the East Coast! I couldn't help myself. But one of them wasn't dead. I thought she'd been stabbed enough. I thought throwing her in the ocean guaranteed another irresistible headline. Shutting her and the police's traps came at a hefty cost. More than I had available. They forced my hand. I was ruined, Henry. Pauperized."

I felt my face turn down in horror. I stared at the gleaming knife in his hand, its sharp cutting edge reflecting the pale light. Our family name was built on murder and deception. I remembered every time I told someone about our family's history. The pride in my voice.

"Don't look so frightened!" he said. "Lots of men have secrets. I've heard some within these walls you wouldn't believe. I'm sure you have your fair share."

"Not like that," I said. "I can't believe this. Let me out of the shower."

"I can trust you to keep this a secret, right, Henry?"

"I don't know," I said. I hadn't gotten that far yet. I was still wrapping my mind around what he'd told me. He gave away the money that should've kept our family wealthy for a long time. *My* money.

"Son. You're not going to ruin our family name, are you?"

"What use is the name now? We live like everyone else. And now I learn you were a murderer? Did you even have heart disease?"

"Pardon me?" he said, bringing a hand to his chest.

"You died of heart disease. Was that a lie, too?"

"I did? That's news to me. Last thing I remember I was out on the balcony, trying to forget the whole mess, enjoying my morning coffee. I will say, it did taste a little funny. My butler said it was a new blend."

"Whatever. It doesn't matter. I'm telling everyone."

"Henry," he pleaded.

I should've been more afraid, but my rage drowned out any other emotion.

"The family deserves to know what happened. We were left with nothing!"

His frown turned into a deranged snarl as he lunged toward me, knife held high, and phased through the glass wall.

I closed my eyes and cowered.

Nothing.

I peeked from behind my arms. He was gone. I stood up and took slow breaths to steady my heartbeat.

The shower head sprayed me with water, soaking my suit.

I tried the handle again, and this time, it opened. I slid on the wet tile floor after putting my entire body weight against the swinging door. I fell with a crash. After gathering myself, I attempted to reach in and turn the water off, keeping as much of myself outside the shower as possible. The knob wouldn't move.

I changed into dry clothes and sat on the bed. I opened my phone and stared at my dad's contact, my thumb hovering over the call icon. A champagne bottle and a single glass sat in an ice bucket on the dresser, enticing me.

I paid a lot of money for this room. This can wait until tomorrow.

The shower head squeaked off. I waited and listened.

I don't care if a hundred ghosts visit me tonight. They'll probably make better conversation than the dolts in the office.

"All done?" I said to the empty room. Nothing.

I turned on the TV to some movie I'd seen before and got into bed. Each time my mind returned to George, I took a swig to try and forget.

He killed all those people. Here.

Drink.

The old hunting knife my dad showed me in Grandma and Grandpa's basement.

Drink.

I pretended to be George during Heritage Day in elementary school. The other kids were so jealous.

Drink.

The entire bottle was almost empty before I passed out.

I had a dream.

Rhythmic waves rocked me. The salty air stung my nose. I remember being at peace.

Something bumped into my arm. I grasped soggy paper and held it in front of me. It was a copy of *The Canal Street Journal.* My fingers traced the headline.

In large, bold letters, it read:

WRIGHT SLAIN
NEWSPAPER ROYALTY FOUND STABBED

The running ink made it impossible to read the article.

As I tossed the dissolving paper aside, I glimpsed the water around me. It was a deep red. I looked down at my floating body.

I'd been stabbed, multiple times.

The old hunting knife was sticking out of my belly.

I reached for the handle, but as soon as I touched it, a bolt of pain snapped me awake.

The harsh morning light burrowed into my aching skull. I rolled over and felt wet sheets. After sniffing my hand, I was relieved to find it smelled of alcohol. The analog clock on the nightstand read 10:30. With a checkout time in thirty minutes, I rushed to gather my things. I swung the door open and hustled to the front desk. The hotel's decor, once charming, now felt phony. The intricate designs of the gaudy fabrics and ornate furniture seemed forced and excessive, lacking the genuine warmth it once held.

"Good morning, sir," the clerk said.

"Morning. Checking out, please," I said, wiping sweat from my forehead.

"Name?"

"Wright. Henry Wright."

The clerk looked up.

"Any relation to George Wright?"

Keller Agre is a horror fiction writer originally from Overland Park, Kansas whose work has appeared in Haunted Words Press and Sirens Call Publications. He is a member of the Atlanta Writers Club as well as various book clubs in the Atlanta area where he lives and works. He enjoys hiking the Appalachian

Mountains, playing folk music on his guitar, and bothering his dog, Banjo.

ANGELS AND SAINTS

BOBBI A. CHUKRAN

Want to hear a spook story?
Well, pardner, belly up to the bar, buy me another drink, and
I'll tell you one—a true tale, or my name ain't Reverend Joshua
Jones.

This time last year, I set out from my little casita here in Santa Fe on a sunny morning in early winter. Riding through the desert gave me inspiration for my sermons, and a chance to have a chin-wag with the Big Guy upstairs. I have a church just outside town, not much to speak of, but my meager flock is eager to hear me preach the gospel. Truth be told, there ain't much else to do on a Sunday in these parts.

I hadn't gone but a few miles before the breeze kicked up, the clouds turned iron-skillet gray, and the temperature plummeted. The roaring winds whistled in my ears.

A coyote howled in the distance, and I pulled my old coat tighter around my neck and spurred my horse on.

That wind, she howled like a banshee and blew the sand straight into my eyes. Those phantom winds can sure spook a fellow, and a horse. No matter how much you believe in our Lord and Savior, you might take a notion that there could be something else out there. Something that would rather you stay home.

If I'd been smart, I'd've pointed my horse back home, but I didn't expect the storm to get as bad as it did. Soon, the strong gusts whipped the sand up into a whirlwind cloud and the sky became blurry, an eerie mist came up from the desert and a dark murk arose that muted everything in my path.

The wind pert near pummeled the stuffin' outta me and I had no notion how long I rode, or how far. The going was slow, and my horse kept turning away from the wind. So it didn't take long to lose my way.

I ended up on an overgrown trail thick with prickly pear, mesquite bush and thorny vines. The blasts of wind grew colder, and stronger, as the trail led deeper into the sagebrush. Snowflakes began to swirl around me in an unusual show of early winter weather.

Although my mouth and most of my face were covered by a bandana, the grit still lodged in the corners of my eyes and lips and slipped down my throat. That desert dust always finds its way in.

It seemed like I wandered for hours in that blizzard. It was a constant struggle to control my poor horse. Exhausted, I dozed in the saddle then woke with a start, no idea where I was.

Knowing I had to find shelter, I sputtered out a short prayer and called to God to help me find my way.

I squinted up my eyes and kept riding. After a spell, I saw small flickering lights in the distance, like lantern light or fireflies. Blinking, I rubbed at my gritty eyes. Was it somebody's campfire? The phantom flames flickered off and on, dancing with the wind.

How odd, I thought.

Just as I despaired of my fate, I caught a whiff of piñon smoke on the air, and I made off in the distance some sort of hulking shape. As I rode closer, I realized it was an adobe home. Quite a large one, to boot.

I thought I knew the location of all the old haciendas and ranch houses in the area, but I didn't recall hearing about one of this size and neither did I ever see one on my travels in this area.

As I got closer, I saw that the ghostly lights were candle stubs enclosed in small burlap bags. Farolitas, they were called. They were used around Christmas along the plaza back in town. There was a long line of them snaking their way up to the entrance of this home. I breathed a short prayer of thanks.

I reined up into the outer courtyard, fell off my horse, stumbled, and finally got my feet under me. Hitching my horse to an iron ring set into the side of a stone water well and trough,

I leaned for a moment up under the shelter of an immense cottonwood tree and miraculously, the wind died down a bit.

Up close, the house was massive—much larger than I had fathomed from a distance. It had the air of abandonment, yet the candles burned bright.

Directly, a rangy man, as thin as a dried-out string bean, emerged from the shadows. I couldn't make out his face, it was hidden by the brim of a large sombrero. He wore dusty chaps over blue denim britches and carried an old railroad lantern.

"*Hola*, mister!" he called. "Where ya'headin'? You all right?"

"Back to Santa Fe!" I yelled. "Wherever the tarnation that is. I'm lost. I almost got blowed to Kingdom come, but this don't look like heaven. Where am I?"

He laughed and shook his head. "Some call this place heaven. Either way, you're a far piece from where you started if you're headin' back to Santa Fe."

"That's what I was afeared of," I said. "Could I ask the time?"

"It's about supper time," he answered.

I realized I'd been wandering in the desert all day. He pointed to a sort of covered opening into a front sheltered courtyard. I crunched down a gravel footpath to the door, following him.

"Welcome to *Las Sombras*," he said, opening an immense, carved wooden door.

Las Sombras. The Shadows.

"Go on inside. I'll tend to your horse, put him someplace safe for the night."

"Much obliged," I said. I entered the hacienda and stood in the entry, stomping some of the sand off my chaps and boots and waited for the old fellow. Before long, he joined me.

As he removed his hat, I saw he was younger than I'd thought. He had a bright pink scar across his face and a patch over one eye.

I tried not to stare. Probably got his injury wrestlin' some bull or ornery horse, I figured

"I thank the Lord I found you when I did," I said. "Is this your home?"

He laughed. "Oh, no, *señor*. I'm just the caretaker." His voice was raspy, like it had been a long time since he'd spoken. "I'm the only one here now," he explained. "Just keepin' an eye on the place while the owners are away. I've known them since I was a boy. They kindly gave me a home when I had none. I like to repay their kindness by helping others. You're welcome to ride out the storm here. Truth be told, I'd like the company, on a night like tonight."

"If you're sure..." I said.

He nodded. "*Si! Si!* You must be freezin'. Come, sit by the fire."

"Much obliged," I said, then followed him to an inner sitting room of sorts, small and cozy.

"I'll go rustle up some grub. It's not much, but it's hot."

"I am a bit hungry," I said.

He grinned. "Ah, it's just a few old rattler buttons and beans."

At that point, anything would do me as long as it was hot. Even rattlesnake tail. I nodded. "That suits me just fine."

He left to dish up the meal and I took the chance to look around the place. Candles flickering in wall-hung carved wooden sconces illuminated the place, giving it a warm glow.

One wall was covered with dozens of carved wooden *santos*—saints and angels both. Some had unusual rustic wings made from large slivers of wood. The flicker of the candlelight gave the illusion they were shuffling back and forth—that the wings were fluttering. I fancied I heard chanting in the distance and the whir of rushing wind.

I shook my head and blinked. I must have sand in my ears, I thought.

The carvings lined the mantle shelf and the extensive bookcases along the walls of the hallway. I noticed a few were detailed, elaborate creations.

But most were simpler.

I had seen similar carvings in the local museum, but never like these—those ones were just rustic, plain carved winged beings. The facial features were crude notches cut in the wood. As I got closer I realized they were the work of a master *santero*. It takes skill to turn a simple piece of wood into a work of art like these. The carvings seemed almost alive.

In the rest of the room, everything was covered in a thick layer of dust. Like it hadn't been occupied in years.

The old caretaker motioned me to the kitchen and pointed to a basin with a pump. I splashed my face with the frigid water and washed my hands.

An immense white cat, old and wobbly with age, sauntered up, trilled at me then hopped on the table.

"Down, you mangy critter," he said, swatting the cat off the table and smiling. "Blanca always shows up when there's food." He poured a saucer of milk for the "mangy critter."

That simple meal was the best food I'd had in ages. It was a feast of succulent beans cooked in some kind of tomato and chile sauce, spicy and warming—sweet and hot at the same time. The rattler meat was tender and flavorful. Handmade tortillas with sweet butter were served on rustic, thick red clay plates. It was almost like he'd expected me, and had held supper.

He didn't say anything when I bowed my head and mumbled my thanks. I looked up and he'd tucked into his food and was already scraping up a mouthful of beans.

We ate quickly and I helped him clear the table. Afterward, we sat by the fire sipping brandy served in fine-cut crystal. Like I said, I'm not a heavy drinker, but on that night, a warm brandy went down just fine.

"I was admiring your *santos* collection." I nodded toward the walls.

"Yes, *sí, sí.* The owners collect them. The missus travels all over, seeking out the santeros. Most of them come from up north, around Taos." He smiled. "Myself, I prefer the simpler carvings."

"Yes, I noticed those, too. Beautiful work," I said, and he grinned.

We stared into the fire, sipping the brandy. The thick adobe walls muffled the sounds of the storm raging outside. I found myself dozing off.

I must have shivered because he got up, opened an old pine trunk and took out a heavy wool blanket to spread over my legs. It was a colorful piece with bright red diamonds, brown stripes and grey lightning bolts. Not a blanket, I realized, but a bit smaller—a heavy rug.

I pulled my chair up a bit closer to the crackling fire. The brandy was doing a fine job of thawing out the rest of my innards. I ran my hand gently over the rug. "Tell me the story of this rug," I said. "Navajo?"

He nodded. "*Sí*, it's Navajo."

I urged him on, and sat back to enjoy the fire and the brandy.

He stared into the fire for a bit, then spoke. "The rug was a wedding gift to the missus from her mother, a Navajo weaver. She died not long after finishing the rug, just a week before the two got married."

"Quite the gift," I said, and he nodded.

"It's her most prized possession. I think she'd let the whole house burn down before she'd let anything happen to that rug. As we all would."

The rough wool, no doubt sheared from a local sheep and spun by hand, was woven in a diamond pattern with brilliant cerise reds that I knew used a dye made from cochineal, a scaly bug that lived on the prickly pear cactus.

From a friend at the local museum, I'd learned that Navajo weavers purposely put mistakes into the rugs to show that they are imperfect human beings. As a man of God, I appreciated the sentiment.

The caretaker finally sat down, then rummaged around in an ancient basket sitting beside his chair. He took out some sort of knife and a small chunk of white wood and commenced carving, squinting with his one good eye and periodically turning the piece this way and that.

It finally dawned on me. "These carvings, they're yours?" I asked, indicating the angels and saints lining the shelves and walls.

He nodded. "*Sí*, most of the simple ones are my creations. I like bringing the wood back to life after it has died. It's cottonwood. Trimmings from the tree outside."

I nodded and watched him carve. It was hypnotic, and it wasn't long before exhaustion overwhelmed me.

The old man chuckled, got up, and motioned for me to follow him. "I'll take you to your room. It's not much, but there's a fire and you won't freeze. Bring the rug with you."

"Oh, no, I couldn't..." I started.

"Don't worry. It's made of sturdy stuff; you can't hurt it. And it will give you good dreams."

He led me down a long hallway to a small room. A crackling fire had already been laid in a rudimentary beehive-type adobe fireplace in the corner. A cowskin rug covered the dark stone floor and a rustic rocking chair sat by the window.

The carved cottonwood angels hanging on the walls of the room gave the impression of flight.

I fell into the small wooden bed, pulled the woolen rug up under my chin and in spite of the howl of a far-off coyote, the rustle of the wind through the cottonwood leaves, and the sand gently pinging against the window, I fell into a deep sleep.

In the middle of the night, I felt the cat jump up on the bed, spin around a few times, then settle at my feet, on top of the rug.

I dreamed of the soft rustle of wings, some whispered chanting and singing and a flurry of angels.

The next morning, I woke up early to the smell of hot coffee. A sliver of sunlight poked through the tiny window high on the wall near the ceiling.

Pulling on my britches and boots, I splashed frigid water on my face from the china basin in the corner.

I followed my nose and after a few wrong turns, found the kitchen.

Although there was hot food and coffee on the table, the woodcarver was nowhere to be seen. Maybe he was outside, tending to some critter or the other.

I ate like a man starved, stuffing myself on scrambled eggs, spicy salsa and fat tortillas.

When I finished, I went to the bedroom to gather my belongings, all of which had already been laid out on the bed. My saddlebags had been wiped clean and my hat had been brushed. The rug was folded neatly at the end, bringing some color to the room.

The little angel the caretaker made last night sat on top of my saddlebags. There was a scribbled note underneath. "A token to remind you of your visit at *Las Sombras. Vaya con Dios.*"

There was also a hand-drawn map, clear enough so I could make my way back home.

Shoving it all in my coat pocket, I grabbed my saddlebags and walked outside, thinking-I might come back later for another visit to talk again with my new friend and see more of the old *hacienda*. The storm had passed and the adobe glowed a warm pink in the sunlight.

My horse was waiting, tied to the front gate. He had been combed and the saddle gleamed.

With one last glance, I swung up into the saddle and headed north. The desert air was crisp and cold at that time of morning. The storm the night before had made the horizon crystal clear.

Using the map, I quickly realized I wasn't far from the trailhead that would lead me home. Like a jackass with his tail on fire, I struck out for Santa Fe.

The next day, I met my museum friend at a little restaurant on the plaza. After the howdys and how-dos were out of the way, we took our seats and ordered.

As the waiter left, I got to the point. "What do you know about the *Las Sombras hacienda?*"

He nodded. "Interesting history there. Why do you ask?"

"I was out there yesterday and got lost in that dad-blamed storm, and the caretaker let me take shelter for the night."

"Hmmm. I wasn't aware that they'd hired a new caretaker," he said. "Not much to see out there now, is there?"

"Oh, I dunno. I thought it quite somethin'. I'd like to learn more of it."

He nodded. "There is a certain beauty in those old abandoned adobes. It's sure not like it used to be, before the fire."

Fire?

I shook my head. "Are you sure we're talkin' about the same place? Maybe another ranch?"

He thought for a moment. "I'm not aware that there are any others in that area."

Then our food was served, several friends stopped by our table to jaw a bit, then the talk turned to the weather, local politics, this and that.

Finally, we were alone again.

"Let's walk over to my office after we're done here," my friend said. "Since you're curious about that old place, I have something to show you. And there's an interesting legend surrounding it you might like. I know how you love stories."

After we ate, we walked across the street to his office, next door to the Governor's Palace.

We sat down and he hesitated for a moment. "We don't know a lot about *Las Sombras*. Wish we did. It was built sometime in the 1880s from handmade adobe. The *vigas*, or pine ceiling poles, were harvested from the forest here and hauled to the home site by a team of mules."

I nodded. "Must have been a sight to see when it was first built."

"I'm sure it was. Unfortunately, there was a fire and the hacienda was all but destroyed. The old well, and some ruins of the walls are all that's left of it. Oh, and there's a grave out behind the house.

"You mentioned a fire?" I asked.

He nodded. "Nobody knows how it got started. Maybe the house was struck by lightning. Some blamed the caretaker, said he'd been smoking in bed or left one of the fireplaces untended."

"But, that can't be," I mumbled.

"What's that?" he asked.

I shook my head. "Nothing. Go ahead, finish the story."

He gave me a peculiar look, then continued. "Most of the house was destroyed, then the fire spread to the barn and other outbuildings. As you know, there's a lot of wood in the ceilings of adobes. The *vigas* are massive, and pine burns hot and fast."

I thought about the beautiful ceiling in the bedroom where I'd spent the night.

My friend continued. "A few neighbors tried to put out the fire, but according to an old timer, it was a beast that raged out of control. Water was limited to one old well and before long, they just gave up and let it burn."

I shook my head, visualizing the blaze and the loss of the treasures inside the hacienda.

But surely this could not be the same place.

"The family, fortunately, was not there, only the caretaker. The story is he ran back inside to save an old cat the owners doted on. They say he wrapped the cat and a photo album in a Navajo rug and carried them to safety."

"What happened to the caretaker?" I asked, not really sure I wanted to know.

My friend shook his head. "Apparently, one of the massive logs fell and hit him in the head. When the family got home later that night, they found him face down in a pile of rubble, his body protecting the rug and photos with their cat sitting by his side. He had a large gash across his face. There was no way he could have survived."

I stared at my friend.

"They buried him on the property... After that, they were never the same. I believe they moved to town for a while, then she moved away after her husband died."

"And you say there's a legend?"

He smiled. "Of course there is. There's always some legend, isn't there? The story goes that when nearby travelers are in need, the caretaker appears to help them. Silly old ghost story, you ask me," he laughed. "As a man of the cloth, I imagine you can take that story with a grain of salt."

"What was his name? The caretaker, who was he?"

He shrugged. "That, my friend, is a fact lost to history. Nobody knows what his name was."

"When was the fire?" I asked.

He frowned, "Oh, if I recollect, it was about a decade back, 1902, somewhere around there. We found some photos and the Navajo rug in an old trunk that was bequeathed to the museum after the husband died. Later on, some woodcarvings appeared in a small parcel, addressed to the museum. We never knew who sent them, but they were attributed to the caretaker. Apparently his hobby was carving *santos*."

"Incredible..." I mumbled.

"Some letters kept by a neighbor helped put some pieces of the puzzle together." He swung around in his chair and pulled out a long, thin drawer. "Take a look at this. We're very lucky to have this piece."

He pulled out a Navajo rug with a bright cerise-red diamond pattern. The rug had faded in spots, but the red coloring was still vibrant.

"Beautiful, isn't it? This is the highlight of the *Las Sombras* collection."

"I've seen this rug before," I whispered.

My friend looked at me as if I'd gone mad. He shook his head. "How could you? This is one-of-a-kind. It's been in storage here for years. We just recently had it cleaned." He smiled. "It took forever to get the cat hair out of it, so I guess that part of the story is true."

He pushed the drawer shut then reached for a leather-bound photo album. "This seems to be the only existing photo of the hacienda owner's mother, the rug weaver."

In the picture, an old Navajo woman sat proudly in a chair in front of a massive loom with the rug draped across it. A man and woman were in the next photo with a cat. Then there was a photo of a younger man with a horse in the hacienda courtyard, underneath the shade of a cottonwood tree. He was fresh-faced, smooth skinned, and wore a huge smile.

And a large sombrero.

In spite of the lack of his scar, I'd recognize him anywhere. The woodcarver, caretaker of *Las Sombras*.

My friend opened another drawer. Nestled on a layer of cot-
ton there were two familiar hand-carved figures—one angel and
one saint. The aged wood was blackened along the edges like it
had been burned.

My friend pointed to the third photo. "Apparently, this was
the maker of these *santos*. It's a miracle they survived the fire."

A chill ran up my arms to the back of my neck, then raced
down my spine.

I thrust my hands in my pockets and gently ran my fingers over
the smooth cottonwood wings of the carved angel the caretaker
gave me.

"Are you sure about this?" I asked.

He shrugged. "As sure as we can be, given the lack of information."

I didn't doubt my friend's story, but something just didn't add
up. This could not be the same family, the same woodcarver or
the same hacienda. Was I going mad, or something else?

Still, as a man of God, I reckoned I knew better than to
scoff at mysterious things that happen in the desert, especially
around Santa Fe. I'd seen my share. People say the land there is
enchanted. I think there's something to that.

Determined to find out for myself, I quickly said my goodbyes
and rode back in the direction of the hacienda, following the
hand-drawn map.

Oddly enough, the other note from the caretaker had disappeared.

Las Sombras was easier to find in the bright, clear daylight, and not nearly as far as it had seemed riding home from my first visit.

As I rode nearer, I reined up my horse and sat, staring at a pile of adobe rubble. Only a few of the massive pine vigas remained, half-buried in sand, and the old well was covered with rotten boards, thorny vines surrounding it. The metal ring where I had tied my horse was rusted through.

Weeds sprouted from the corners of the courtyard, and I was sorrowed to see the magnificent cottonwood had fallen.

A dusty path snaked around to the back of the house, where I hadn't ventured two days before.

In a weed-choked area enclosed in rusted wrought iron, I found an old stone grave marker. I took out my kerchief and wiped away the thick layer of dust that hid the carving on the front.

A gust of wind snaked down my collar and someone whisper my name. I whipped around but there was no one.

I stooped closer to read the inscription.

Here lies our trusted friend, caretaker, and maker of angels and saints, who gave his life caring for others. His spirit lives on in his work. 1860 - 1902.

I tried to remember the caretaker's name, but oddly, don't recollect that he ever told me. According to this, he had died years ago.

Who was he? What was he? Angel? Saint? Ghost? I stood at his grave and whispered a little prayer for his soul.

Bobbi A. Chukran lives in a small West Texas town where she tends an enchanted garden and cavorts with the occasional chupacabra, cactus-eared jackrabbit and raucous rattler. A fourth-generation native Texan, she has lived and traveled extensively in the Southwest, where she's met a few ghosts.

Bobbi writes short fiction--speculative, mysterious and nefarious. Her work has been published in Black Cat Weekly, Kings River Life, Dark Eclipse, Over My Dead Body!, Mysterical-E, the Dead Mule School of Southern Literature and numerous anthologies. She has one collection of macabre fiction/poetry, HALLOWEEN THIRTEEN. She is also an award-winning youth playwright, specializing in (sometimes dark) comedy re-tellings of folk and fairy tales, including THE JOURNAL OF MINA HARKER.

www.bobbichukran.com

HER FACE

LAURA BOHLCKE

The crowd jostled, shoulders rubbing, hands pushing, trying to get a look at Her face.

Serene and still, her expression was a stark contrast to the noise and chaos of the dirty London street that pulsed on the other side of her pollution-streaked window. She'd hung there for days, her sightless plaster eyes gazing out on a near constant stream of humans, horses, and carriages. But even with the vast number of gawkers, not a soul had come forward with information about who she was in life—or how she met her death.

It was common for the coroner to make a plaster mold of a nameless corpse's face. Often times, that death mask would bring the much-needed identification of the dead. It was normal for people to stop in passing and gaze at the frozen face behind the smudged glass, but this mask, this woman, was different. Her face drew admiring crowds who did not come to bring her a name, but only to stare through the window, transfixed by her tranquility.

Pulled from the Thames two days prior, the coroner had determined the young woman had been strangled and drowned. But even with the horrific nature of her death, her face was frozen in a soft smile with relaxed eyes that made her seem at peace with her fate. He had lingered over her body longer than most—captivated by the gentle brown curls, handsome feminine curves, and delicate features. The coroner thought she couldn't have been more than twenty, and guessed from her clothes that she must have worked in one of the many factories...or had just come to London to find work. As he ran his finger along her cheek, he pictured how pink it must have looked in life. He had known then, that even after her body was identified and carried away, he would keep his plaster mold of her face for himself.

But as the days passed with no name for his poor Jane Doe, the fervor over her death mask increased. When the first aristocrat in a silk vest and top hat graced his dank autopsy room in an attempt to buy her face, the enterprising coroner knew he had a moneymaking operation on his hands.

In the dark of his basement, he filled the mold with plaster, and made death mask after death mask.

A neat row of restful duplicates of her face.

She wasn't sure what had pulled her from the warm comfort of her veiled sleep, but when she opened her eyes she found herself surrounded by dark. She had the sensation of floating, but could feel nothing. Nothing at all.

Hello?

Her voice was small in the vastness of the nothing.

Where am I?

With the deepness of her sleep slipping away, her rising fear changed from where she was...to who she was. As she drifted, all she could remember were bright flashes of moments, but nothing that could be called memories.

Hello?

The Dark swirl surrounded her, circling her for a moment before starting to push—or was it pull—her through the emptiness. Twisting and waving, she tried to stop her movement across the void, but The Dark was far too strong to be resisted.

See

The voice of The Dark rumbled inside her as two small points of light glittered in the distance. Transfixed, she stopped fighting The Dark and let it push her closer. As she glided to a stop, she realized what she was looking at were holes.

Holes in the void.

See

Obeying The Dark, she pushed her face up to the holes. The spacing fit her eyes perfectly.

Candlelight danced over rich upholstery and polished wood surfaces. Her mind was filled with the sounds of laughter and clinking glasses. Voices very close talked of a tragic life cut short.

I remember something. I remember hands on my neck.

"As soon as I saw Margret and Ashland's mask, I just knew we had to have one." A woman in a dark gray dress was looking right at Her. "Sweet Face...that's what everyone is calling her now."

A memory of ice-cold water burst into her mind, snapping her away from the candlelit room and back into the nothing. A memory of moving water with the moon shining overhead as she sank, drowning into death.

Dead! Oh, God! I remember dying. I'm Dead!

Holding her hands out before her in the flicker of light from the holes, she shrieked in horror at her transparency, her formlessness.

Please no! Please, I can't be dead.

Dead

The Dark whirled around her and once again began to drag her spirit through the void. Spinning through the black, she heard more voices, saw more candlelight gleaming out of holes in the nothing. She drifted toward the brightness of a new room.

"Gawd. Can ya believe this thing?" A woman in a black dress and crisp white apron was staring into Her eyes.

Behind her, a young man in an ill-fitting coat and dirty cap was stacking wood by an ornate fireplace. "Come away from that, Bessy. She's bad luck, that one."

Bessy shrugged. "Wouldn't want my face made into a mask and sold to the posh to hang on a wall after I'm dead. Just not natural."

From her side of the fracture, she called out to the man and the woman in the world of the living. Screamed to them for help. But they couldn't hear her and went on about their tasks. Behind her, The Dark tugged and she slipped back into the void.

I don't understand what's happening. Please, please tell me what's happening.

Your Face

What?

Your Face

As frightful comprehension washed over her; she felt as though she might drift apart with grief.

It's my face on the wall? My face made into a mask and hung on display?

Your Face

But why? Why would they do that?

She turned back to the holes in the nothing and saw the gentle almond shape of her own eyes.

How could they do such a thing?

In the center of her being, she felt the now familiar pull of The Dark. Yielding control, she flowed through the abyss. Ahead she heard sounds from another house, other voices. She spun toward them. Understanding now, her spirit pressed up against the back of her death mask and peered out into the new room.

A stout man was pouring whiskey into a round glass. Turning to a thinner man seated in a red velvet chair, he gestured toward her with his drink. "The police still have no idea who she is or who could have killed her."

Oh My God—they are talking about me. But how can the police have no idea? I went to them when he first threatened me. Told them...didn't I?

"Cannot imagine she was up to any good." The thin man drained the wine from his glass. "Coming to an end like that...not the sort of thing that happens to proper people."

Proper? Was I not proper?

She remembered speaking to a man in uniform. A man who shrugged and ignored her fear.

I told them! I asked for help! Why did no one help me? Please...you can't say these things about me. I was good. I know I was.

As she shrank back from the horror of their words, The Dark took hold of her again and hauled her through the nothing toward her face in a new room. What little confidence she'd had in life was being ripped away by the sneering voices that knew nothing of who she had tried her best to be.

"I heard she was pregnant with a married noble's bastard and he killed her to protect his good name."

Fake gasps made their way to her phantom ears. The Dark reached out again and she surrendered, allowing the force to move her at its will.

They don't care. Not about me, not about what happened...not about the pain their words and joyous speculation cause.

"They are saying she was a prostitute who fell in love with a client and then took her own life when the man rejected her."

I would never. I had so few options...as a woman I was dependent on others for what little I could scrape together for myself...but I would never.

She felt the cold grip of The Dark as it latched onto her again, dragging her through the vast emptiness to another room.

How many faces of mine are there?

The Dark didn't answer, but she could feel them out there in the nothing like star points all around her. Their existence made her feel stretched and thin.

Fire crackled in the room as she pressed to a new mask. Sprawled on disheveled sheets, four naked bodies writhed to an exhilarated finish and collapsed in a pile of heavy breathing. A man with blonde hair plastered to his pale forehead lifted his face from the bosom of the woman beneath him and gestured toward the mask on the wall.

"Do you think she enjoyed the show?"

The woman beneath him pulled his head back down to her. "Probably learned a few things."

"Nothing she can use now that she's food for worms." A man with dark hair sat up and reached for a drink on the table next to the bed.

"I think it's creepy to have Sweet Face just staring down at us." The final member of the tangle of flesh took the glass from the dark-haired man and touched it to her lips.

"Nonsense," the dark haired man said. "I think it's magnificent."

How can they steal my face and treat me like a curiosity? I am a person...was a person. They have no right to me.

She turned and pushed herself back into the nothing, storming toward another room under her own power— no need for a pull from The Dark.

"Alistair says the police have given up the hunt for who might have done her in." Smoke billowed from the man's fat cigar.

"Probably a runaway, anyway. Maybe from a wealthy family...wouldn't that be the thing? Killed by a lover under the cover of night," the cigar smoker's friend gurgled into his bourbon.

They have no concern for truth or honor. Every day was a struggle against those who believed they had a right to me...to my autonomy, to my thoughts, to my body. And now they claim me even in death.

Her insecurities burned into anger as she slipped again into the nothing and found another mask.

"Such a peaceful countenance." A woman with a feather in her hat regarded her face in a room with wide windows that looked out on a green lawn.

I am not peaceful. Not anymore. I am not the mask.

A new room. A new woman in a dress with a high lace collar. "Well of course Henry and I have a Sweet Face mask. We absolutely had to get one. They are all the rage."

All. The. Rage.

The lace-collared woman and her gaggle of friends tittered and took turns making guesses about how Sweet Face had died.

As she listened to their gruesome tales, her indignation twisted into hate. Even after the voices of that house had fallen silent and the candles had gone out, she brooded behind her plaster visage. To the deepest corner of her soul, she felt how powerless she had been in life and seethed about finding herself even more so in death. Wealthy people with no understanding of what it meant to struggle dared to use her for their fleeting amusement.

I need them to stop.

Malice coiled and uncoiled in her heart like smoke.

How do I make them stop?

In the hush of the house, the force of her rage poured from the death mask like a cloud and hovered in the air before her face. Bringing order to her disorder, she willed her essence back into its familiar shape: shoulders, legs, torso, and head. She looked down at her floating form. her dress, its once coarse fabric now soft as the breeze, fluttered in the stillness. Satisfied, she stretched out one glorious spectral arm and then the other. As she turned her head from side to side, her now white curls twirled buoyantly about her as though uplifted by unfelt winds.

An apparition of animosity, she hung in the air rejoicing in her newfound freedom. But the newness itself created a challenge. With no physical form, she had no idea how to move about the room. First she tried using her ghost legs to walk like she had in life, but that proved useless. She continued to dangle in the same spot.

Walking used to be as easy as breathing...and now I can't do either.

But the notion of breathing resonated with her spirit form. Lung-less, she drew the energy of the room around her into her being and then let it out. The action slid her through the air with ease. A few minutes of practice allowed her to guide her movements, use the currents of the room's ebb and flow to propel herself in the direction she wanted to go.

Let's find the lady of the house.

Riding a stream of air, she went hunting for the woman with the high lace collar.

I will explain...tell her she's hurting me. Get her to tell the others.

Up the stairs to the wide landing and down the long hall, she let her instincts carry her. At each heavily closed door she would ease her body through the wood and survey the room on the other side. At last she found her prize. Sleeping next to the snoring Henry, the woman with the high lace collar lay with her head on an embroidered pillow.

Hovering in the doorway, her white gauze form rippled in a room with no breeze. As she tried to think of the words to say to convince the woman with the high lace collar that delighting in the suffering of another was wrong, the woman stirred in bed and sat up. Instantly the lavish bedroom rang with the woman's screams. Shrieking, she clutched at her husband as he snorted awake. Wild with fear, the woman stabbed her finger in the direction of the apparition. Henry choked on the image of her and struggled to free himself from the bedclothes and get to his feet.

As the couple panicked, she realized in her own horror that she couldn't tell them anything. Her wizened lips moved, but only silence came out. She had a fleeting feeling of hopelessness as she sagged in the air. But the previous jests of the woman screaming in the bed came back to her and her feelings of despair were overcome by the burning of her indignation.

If they can't hear my words, then they will have to hear my actions.

By now, Henry stood in the center of the room brandishing a fire poker at her while his wife cowered in the bed.

"Kill it, Henry!"

Kill me? HA! Maybe I should kill you?

With the heat of her outrage roiling off her in waves, she knew she must be a terrible thing to behold. Unfortunately, she was not lucky enough to have her victims collapse from fright. She would have to do them in herself.

But as she lingered on this precipice of revenge, she faced another problem she had not considered. In her formless state, she had no weapon to wield against her enemies.

Perhaps...

Again she breathed in the room, striving to calm her violent mind. Measured and slow, she breathed the world back out. Lifting her ghost hands, she focused on her dull rounded fingertips with their ghastly white cracked nails. With each deliberate intake of energy from the space around her, she compelled those fingertips to lengthen, sharpen, and hone themselves to fine points until they were no longer fingers at all.

Straightening her ghost hands, she grinned at the stinging claws she'd made. Drawing in one more time, she focused all her strength on making her ghost talons solid. She shuddered as she pushed her anger down through her arms to the spikes that gleamed like metal in the dark.

Raising her face to the poker-waving Henry, she knew he and his ridiculous wife were helpless before the fierceness of her rage. Gliding forward, she advanced on her prey. Crumpling, Henry dropped his weapon and retreated to the far wall. As a test, she dragged the tip of one claw along the wooden post of her quarry's bed. Like a knife through butter, her claw carved a groove in the wood.

Sliding across the bed, she turned on the woman with the high lace collar. The woman still screamed and gripped the useless bedclothes for protection. Levitating above the prone woman, she stretched out one single sharpened finger and scratched a line of blood down the side of the woman's face—down her face and along her neck to her chest. Startled by pain, the woman's hand flew to her face, her eyes fixed on the phantom above her. Hair flying, eyes on fire with fury, grasping claws outstretched, she imagined she was the most horrible thing that woman had ever seen.

She moved in close, the cold of her freezing the woman in her bed. Swiping shallow at the long exposed throat, she wanted the woman with the high lace collar to understand she was going to die. Know like she had known...and be powerless to stop it. The complete terror in the woman's eyes thrilled her. The next stroke of her claws was deep and final.

Perhaps we should make a mask of your dead face and make jokes about your virtue now that you have no voice to defend yourself, hmmm?

The soundless words from her gray lips left ice crystals on the dying woman's ear.

As the woman with the high lace collar breathed her last, the angry ghost turned on her shrinking husband. With barely a glance at the bloody mess that had been his wife, he scrambled to his feet and made for the door. A plan forming in her now wicked mind, she let him run. Back down the hall. Back down the stairs. She pursued his fleeing form to the room where they had hung her face. In full view of her death mask, she brought him down like a rogue beast and left him to bleed out on his imported rug.

Her night's work done, she found she was threadbare tired. She returned to her place in the void to await morning.

As the house awoke, she delighted in the screams ringing off the walls. Policemen and important men in long coats bustled around the room making proclamations about leaving no stone unturned till they had found the fiend responsible for such a horrific act.

You didn't turn over any stones to find what happened to me, did you?

She watched the police blunder around in their impotency for a while before deciding it was time to go. As she allowed The Dark to pull her back into the nothing, she extended one of her sharp talons and tapped the backside of the replica of her face. The sound of it smashing to the ground rang as she pushed past The Dark in search of her next victim.

The stout man. What a picture he will be after I've ripped open that ample gut with my shiny new claws.

He was asleep in his chair before the fire, a glass dangling in his hand, when she found him. Wrath in her heart, she surged from her mask and glided to him on the room's currents. She felt stronger tonight, more solid. A candle burned on the table beside him. As she passed her gossamer hand through its flame, she was delighted by the taste of its heat in her mouth. Circling his slumped form, she extended one sharp finger. With the slightest swipe, she cut first one button and then another from his too-tight vest.

Plink.

Plink.

The buttons bounced across the tiled floor.

Plink.

Another button went flying. He stirred from his drunken sleep, a hand going to where the open vest had exposed his shirt. Grunting, he tried to sit up, dropping his glass with a splintering crash.

"Damn." His head lolled in the direction of his ruined drink.

She circled, extending the rest of her razor fingers.

As he shook off having broken the glass and rolled his head back toward the ceiling, he caught sight of her. "What?"

He floundered to his feet, immediately tumbling to the floor under his own weight. Feeling his fear like a tonic, she bore down on him. Graceless, he scrambled backward across the floor. But she was too fast for him to escape. His breath came out like winter as she let her phantom skirts drape across him. Firelight glinted off her raised claws. With a flash, she ripped through his wrinkled shirt and into his soft white flesh. His mouth made a few sloshing sounds and then he fell still.

"Not the sort of thing that happens to proper people, is this?" Her voice came out this time, but was more sand than sound.

For a time she spun in the air above him and relished her feeling of control, but then the spark of a thought burst into her mind.

What fun it would be to leave them a hint. A lesson for the living from the undignified dead.

A smile spreading across her grim pale face, she unfurled her claws again. Slicing in an uneven oval, she removed the skin of his face with careful cuts. Once she had the fleshy thing in her hands she drifted about, looking for the right place to exhibit her treasure. When she saw the bust of some man in the main entryway, she knew it was perfect. She draped the skinned face over the stone face so that someone entering the house would see it straight away.

Pleased with her work, she retreated to her mask to watch the discovery unfold.

It was all she could have hoped for. A maid raised the alarm just after sunrise as she entered and found her master's face on display. Her shouts brought the rest of the household staff, and then the police.

Again the authorities paced and sweated as they took in the gory scene.

Again they had no inkling who could have committed this heinous murder.

No one even considered the idea that it had been carried out by a dead woman who had been strangled and drowned and now floated behind her death mask watching them.

When the stout man's body had been carried away and all that was left was the maid trying to clean his blood from the floor, she smashed this house's version of her face and fell back into the warm familiarity of the void. Around her, The Dark rumbled. A rolling sound like deep laughter. Knowing it enjoyed her revenge as well, she let it lead her to back to another home with her face.

The two naked couples lay draped over each other in a tangle of arms and legs in the large overstuffed bed. Exhausted from their lovemaking, not a one of them stirred when a cloud of shadow emerged from the mask on the wall and coalesced into a fearsome ghostly figure. Content to take it slow, she floated around the room—wondering at the opulence of the place.

Catching a glimpse of her ghost face in the gold-framed mirror, She cackled.

I am not tranquil anymore. I am not the mask.

When she was done, the four naked bodies lay sprawled around the room—their limbs twisted, grotesque gashes covering their flesh in blood. She placed their faces in a neat row on the intricately carved dresser.

When the police came to study the crime scene, she grew bored watching. But when one of the inspectors in a long coat stopped in front of her face and gazed up, her heart leapt.

"Cooper. This mask...there was one at each of the other two murder scenes, wasn't there?"

She vibrated with excitement.

"Yeah...there were. But both those are broken now. Went back for follow-up questions and each was lying on the floor in shards."

The inspector *humphed* and continued to regard the mask. "I wonder what that connection means?"

With her eyes locked on his through the plaster, she tapped the back of the mask with her pointed finger and returned to the void as it cracked and fell. Whisking along to the next mask, she wished she could have seen his reaction.

Each night she repeated her performance. Houses with her face on the wall were visited in the wee hours of the night by a fiend that would rip the owners open wide, place the skin of the victims' faces on display, and leave without a trace. Each morning as she broke the mask of her face and left, she found she felt stronger.

It was only toward the end that she began to hear the people in the rooms whisper their suspicions that Sweet Face might be to blame. First it was hushed conversations in corners by people unwilling to be seen as crazy or superstitious, but as her campaign continued, even the police were beginning to speculate that something supernatural could be at work. The believers that owned a Sweet Face smashed their masks and threw away the pieces, saving themselves from her talons. But others laughed off such rubbish and continued to display her face...until she wafted into their bedrooms and sliced their bellies.

At last, only one more room called to her in the emptiness of the veil. Dark and dank, so different from the wealthy homes she had splattered with blood, the coroner's rooms were modest at best. As she swirled from the last mask, he was looking right at her. Stunned, he staggered back, knocking over items on his desk.

"You." He pressed his back to the wall. "It was you that killed all those people, wasn't it? You used the masks, didn't you?"

She showed her teeth in a half-smile, half-grimace as She skimmed across his dusty floor. Gone was the flowing gauzy ghost that had first emerged from the mask. Now she was charcoal gray and able to topple furniture as she raged across a room.

"But you...you won't hurt me. Without me there would be no mask for you to move through. I...you are my Sweet Face."

Her voice came dry and guttural as she flared out her fingers for a final time and raked them across his body. "It is *My* face."

Laura Bohlcke (pronounced Bowl-Key) is a writer who has spent the last 30 years working in the film industry making television commercials. While assisting clients and agencies in their efforts to sell their mayonnaise or bubbly beverages is a wonderful way to keep a roof over her head, Laura is also intent on telling stories of her own and makes time to write every day. In her home in Texas she can be found in an office filled with oddities and curiosities dreaming up tales of horror to share with the world or out in the sunshine tending to her extensive garden with her giant dog and feral cat.

ROADSIDE MEMORIAL

ANDY COE

Three miles south of the highway on County Road 117, there is a roadside memorial. It is nothing extravagant: a colorful assortment of flowers cradling a small cross planted in the cold earth. Affixed to the cross's intersection is a plaque that reads: *You're home now, Honey Bear. Lydia Grace Mitchell, 6/22/85 - 9/10/95.*

Contrary to what the plaque states, Lydia Mitchell is far from home.

She stands by this lonely memorial now, watching the occasional car roll by. Vehicles do not appear often—but then again, perhaps they do. The passage of time is a strange thing for Lydia: a smeared blur of partial thoughts and indistinct memories that only gains clarity with the sudden approach of life, or when she attempts to remember the moment she died.

If she tries, she can faintly smell the earthy scent of the impending rain that loomed in the clouds. Taste the cloying remnants of the Double Chocolate Oreo milkshake she'd had from the Dairy Shack. And if she really concentrates, she can even feel a slight twinge in her lower back where she'd slammed into the telephone pole. She's glad it only manifests as a twinge now; it was much more on that black night.

Lydia Mitchell is only ten years old, but wise beyond those years. Wise enough to understand that because of what happened to her she will *always* be ten. Wise enough to understand she is dead and has been for a good long while.

While those occasional passing cars snap her out of the fog of unknowing that blankets her, they never hold her attention. Nor does she enjoy lingering on the fading sensations of her last moments on earth. However, she enjoys her two visitors. They are like a hot beam of sunlight in her fog, temporarily burning it away to reveal the curious mind of the girl she used to be.

One of those visitors arrives now, and the ghost of her once-beating heart seems to quicken as his car pulls onto the shoulder of the road opposite her memorial. The man behind the wheel keeps the engine running, as he always does, and wisps of exhaust trail from the tailpipe to dissolve into the summer heat. From the gravel shoulder on her side of the road, Lydia looks into his weary eyes. The man, in turn, looks *through* hers.

She knows he can't see her; he is only gazing upon the planted cross and assorted flowers. But while she has learned to resist the urge to run across the road to him (such a feat is impossible, as she is bound to the roadside shrine), that urge remains. Lydia wants to throw her arms around the man, tell him that she misses him.

Tell him she loves him.

The man behind the wheel—Charles Mitchell, her father—begins to speak. His words are silent behind the rolled-up window, but Lydia can feel the pain, sorrow, and anger bleeding off him. She wonders, as she does with every visit, why her mother is not there with him. He's hurting. She wishes he would simply get out of the car, cross the road, and come to her. Then she might be able to help him. They could help each other.

But Charles Mitchell doesn't get out of his car. He never does. His silent words spoken, he wipes the corner of his eye with a finger, puts the car back in gear, and drives away. He takes his pain, sorrow, and anger with him.

Lydia watches the car shrink down the lonely strip of county road until the fog swallows it. She knows he will eventually be back, and the solemn sequence of events will repeat, but it will be a while. Time is an abstract thing in this shadow reality Lydia now exists within, but—if she were to guess—she thinks her father comes once every summer, on her birthday.

This occurrence marks seven visits.

Seven visits, seven summers.

Seven years dead.

She sees her second visitor more often.

This second visitor offers Lydia her next reprieve from the endless shadow realm when his car pulls off the road a short distance away. The last slivers of sunlight hide his vehicle in the indigo gloom of twilight.

When Lydia sees his tall, slim shape emerge from the murk and approach her modest domain, she knows she should fear him. She should *hate* him with every ounce of her being. He is, after all, the reason she will never turn eleven.

But she doesn't fear him, nor does she hate him. Not anymore.

Gregory Wayne begins the ritual he's performed every few weeks for the past couple of years. He seats himself cross legged on the yellowed grass next to the memorial. He clicks on a palm-sized flashlight once he is comfortable and shines it on the small plaque affixed to the cross.

"Hi, Lydia," he says after clearing his throat. "Sorry for being a little later than usual. Work kept me." Gregory cannot know that the concept of punctuality is alien to Lydia in her strange half-world. Nor can he know his little beam of light is shining directly upon her.

Logic tells her she shouldn't bother, but Lydia answers him anyway. "It's okay, Greg. I'm glad you came."

"Been working a lot, lately, to be honest. Keeps my mind off other things that aren't going so well."

"My dad showed up earlier. He still won't get out of the car. He won't come close to me like you do."

"Had a big fight with Cynthia. She still won't let me see Kayla. And—can you believe this—my little girl doesn't even know I exist. She's never been told."

"Thanks for bringing the extra flowers last time. I really liked having them around."

This pair of one-sided conversations continues for a handful of minutes, with neither participant picking up the thread the other has woven. As she listens to him vent his life's ups and downs, Lydia thinks there is little exaggeration in his claim that things haven't been going well. The circles beneath his eyes are deeper than usual; a bristly patch of stubble has begun to cover his narrow cheekbones; and, if she is not mistaken, there are a few wisps of gray along the part line of his sandy blond hair she does not think were there before.

Eventually, she cannot think of anything else to say to him. Overcome by the sudden urge that always takes her when she is with Gregory, Lydia extends a small, pale hand and touches his shoulder. The effect is immediate, and before she knows it she's—

—driving erratically down Foster Road. Sure, he's thrown back more than a few tonight, but Greg is a seasoned pro at driving while loaded; shit, he could do it with his eyes closed. But the real bitch of it is, driving with his eyes closed is exactly what it feels like he's doing.

This is why I'll always be a city boy, he thinks as he white-knuckles the wheel but continues to stubbornly forge ahead at forty miles an hour. *I can't be more than five miles outside town and it's already so goddamn dark. No streetlamps, no house lights, not even the—*

Greg's train of thought is broken when the T-intersection he's been anticipating jumps out at him from the impenetrable gloom. He lets the car idle in the middle of the intersection as he takes a few moments to compose himself, then turns left onto CR 117.

Just so dark.

The car's speed begins to slowly increase again, almost in direct correlation with the slowing of his heart rate as Greg mentally recovers from his near off-road experience. Soon the speedometer has crept over thirty-five miles an hour. And while it's still a total bitch to see where he's going, he's no longer as concerned about it. That warm, pleasant buzz between his ears is letting his mind wander back to an hour earlier when he'd been in the VIP room of Jaybird's.

What an amazing time it had been; he's glad he'd let Tom talk him into it. A seemingly endless supply of foaming mugs to guzzle down and small bills to stuff into insubstantial thongs had been just what he'd needed to help him forget the persistent headache that was Cynthia. He just needs to make it back home—again, not a problem for a seasoned pro like himself—and he'll be free to hit the pillow and get lost in his debauched, liquor-fueled dreams. If only it wasn't so fucking *dark—*

The shape appears out of the gloom much faster than the T-intersection had.

He has no hope of stopping or swerving.

He hits this unknown shape at thirty-four miles an hour, then continues into a telephone pole, which halts him completely. His head begins to pound from making violent contact with the steering wheel, and the blood streaming from the resultant laceration blurs his vision. Yet this injury also burns away enough of the booze-fog to present a terrible revelation: he's been driving all this time with his lights off.

Just so dark

(a seasoned pro at driving while loaded)

So goddamn dark

His hand shoots to the light switch. When he flips it on, the second revelation hits him like a sledgehammer to the chest.

The shape he's struck with his car is a person.

A little girl.

Greg spends what feels like years frozen in place, pounding head utterly forgotten. Through the haze of smoke from the car's engine, he takes in details.

Her eyes, darting wildly across the grisly scene. Trying to absorb and process what has just happened.

Her pink-striped shirt, blooming with blood. Her body below the waist completely hidden (*consumed*) by the two-ton vehicle and telephone pole pinning her in place.

Glittering shards of bike reflector, scattered across the puckered hood. A reflector that surely would have caught his eye, had he been sober enough to remember his lights.

After uncounted centuries, his paralysis finally breaks. He fumbles with the release latch on his seatbelt, and his legs buckle beneath him as he attempts to stand. Greg crawls around to the front of the vehicle just in time to witness the girl's final moments.

He asks her if she is all right, if she can hear him. But the girl cannot answer. Her darting eyes stop blinking, and her hitching breaths begin to slow. Greg can't help but notice how the slowing of her breath synchronizes with the rattling shudders of the dying car engine. They both stop at nearly the same moment.

Greg can't think of what else to do, so he reaches out a trembling hand and touches the girl. He regrets it almost immediately, and—

—she pulls back when the memory becomes too much. But she does not let go. Instead, Lydia refocuses and grasps for the memory she really seeks. One more recent, and far less personal to her. She finds it, and—

—shakes her head wearily. "Sorry, Greg. I just don't think so."

Greg is at a loss for words; he hadn't expected this. "It's been *seven years*, Cynthia," he says finally. "Seven years sober."

"I get that," his ex-wife replies. She looks tired. Tired of raising a daughter for seven years as a single mother. Tired of this ancient conversation. "But five of those years have been in prison. The other two have been on parole. All *forced* sobriety, Greg. You're being monitored. If no one was watching, you'd slip right back off, Greg. I know you."

Her words slice into him deeply. "Thanks for the vote of confidence."

She only repeats her previous statement. "I know you."

"Then let's forget about a visit for now," Greg offers, desperate to find purchase in this precarious argument. "Let me talk to her on the phone, so I can hear her voice. I just want to get to know her any way I can."

There is a long silence between them. Greg braces himself for what will come next, but he isn't ready when it does.

"That can't happen."

"Why the hell not?" he demands, darting forward in his seat; Cynthia flinches in response.

"Kayla...thinks you're dead."

"What?"

"I told her you died in an accident," she says, unable to meet Greg's piercing gaze. "Figured it was better than her getting to know you, then being crushed when she eventually sees the kind of man you really—"

"You *bitch*!" Greg shoots up from the table, nearly knocking it over.

"Look. She doesn't even remember you, and—"

—Lydia breaks the connection, unwilling to hear the rest. Gregory jerks backward, dropping his little flashlight into the yellowed grass. He is breathless with a sudden surge of inexplicable emotion. They partake in this strange dance—delicate contact, followed by violent separation—nearly every time they meet.

It's not that Lydia particularly enjoys reliving the moment of her death. Often, she chooses to remove her hand from Gregory because if she were to linger too long in those snapshots of the past, she would transition from his memories to her own. What little she remembers of that night is vague and benign: getting into an argument with Tammy and deciding not to spend the night at her house after all; downing most of her milkshake in a few spiteful gulps; and pedaling home with an ice-cream headache, diligently staying within the boundary of the dark road's gravel shoulder. She doesn't remember hearing the car coming up behind her. Doesn't remember wondering why it sounded so close, yet she saw no lights. Doesn't remember thinking, as she was thrown from her bike seat: *I should have had Dad pick me up.* It's for the best that she can't accurately recall those last horrid details, and she prefers to keep it that way.

Rather, Lydia cannot help peering inside Gregory Wayne's head because of the insight it gives her into who he is. Yes, through a simple touch she has seen herself die more times than she can accurately recall. But she has also glimpsed other moments of his life. Small snippets of both good times and bad, which have slowly shifted her opinion of her killer.

Lydia doesn't always understand the more complex and grown-up thoughts and emotions Gregory experiences in these life snippets. But she understands enough to have come to the belief, after all their time spent together, that Gregory Wayne is ultimately a good person. Flawed, but good.

He never meant to take the life of a ten-year-old girl.

He never meant to ruin another father's life by taking away his daughter.

It is because of this belief that she reaches out to him again. Over time her connection with him has turned her into something of a spiritual recorder of sorts; she is able to effortlessly recall most of the memories she has viewed through Gregory, as long as they remain close. Lydia now uses this stored recall to initiate a sort of playback within Gregory. She filters through those memories until she finds the one she wants.

The recollection she chooses is one he shared with her not long ago. Greg is among a group of men, one link in a semicircular chain of steel folding chairs. His chest is warm with pride, with hope for the future. In the palm of his hand is a bronze coin, commemorating another anniversary of freedom. Upon its surface are etched the words "To Thine Own Self Be True." As Greg slowly sinks into the memory, Lydia feels his anguish begin to drain, little by little. Despite the adversity he has faced today, the vision of the coin reminds him that, though there may be many miles ahead, he will eventually reach his destination. He only needs to take it one step at a time.

This is their dance in full: the initial touch that absorbs the pain, the doubt, the anger; and the second touch that delivers the cure. Peace. It is a dance Lydia wishes she could perform with her father.

"I...I think I should probably be going now," Gregory states when the memory of his AA anniversary meeting finally fades. He looks a little dazed from the experience, but he looks *better*.

Gregory grabs his flashlight, stands, then touches the planted cross. "Thanks, Lydia. Visiting you always seems to clear my head. Until next time."

Greg returns two nights later. He does not show up in his car but shambles out of the darkness on unsteady feet.

His business-casual attire is askew: his button-down shirt is half-tucked, and something has spilled on one leg of his dress pants. His sandy blond hair is corkscrewed and untamed. His cheeks are wet with tears. Lydia takes a step backward as he stumbles into range; she's uncertain if she wants to touch him just yet.

Gregory collapses in a defeated heap before the cross. He does not pull out his flashlight. He simply lowers his head into his hands and begins to sob.

Lydia takes another step back. Gregory Wayne's visits have, by and large, always been a comfort to her; she's never seen him like this before.

It scares her.

Because she has no life experience beyond the age of ten, Lydia is unable to identify the unpleasant, cloying odor coming from him as single malt whiskey.

"I keep trying to be better," Gregory says between hitching sobs. "But the universe is against me. It's always fucking *against* me!"

Lydia feels her hand creep outward toward him; she wants to assuage this new pain, as she has so many of his other pains—but she's not sure she wants to see what her touch will reveal.

"I felt better after I talked to you last time," he mumbles as he struggles to get his emotions in check. "I really did. It's just that...I need to see Kayla. Show her that her dad's still alive, and he's not a piece of shit, you know? I should have come back here sooner...talked things through with you again. But I didn't. I decided to grab a few drinks instead, and fucking throw away every bit of progress I've made! Not only that, I—"

Greg's words are cut short by the sudden flash of headlights.

The car pulls forward until it idles in the middle of this lonely stretch of County Road 117, and Gregory flinches in the glare of its headlamps like a convict caught in a prison watchtower spotlight.

Lydia knows who will emerge from the car before she sees him.

Charles Mitchell explodes out the driver's side door with a salvo of expletives. Unlike Gregory, his stride is not shambling, but purposeful. A gun waves dangerously from one extended arm.

"I knew it!" he booms into the still night. "I fucking *knew* you'd come here!"

Greg scrambles to his feet, clumsily trampling some of the memorial's floral arrangements as he does so. "Look—I'll go, man. I'll go!" he stammers. "Just put the gun down, please! I'll get in my car, and you'll never see me—"

Charles Mitchell's thunderous anger drowns out the other man's assurances. "Here I am, sitting in the Pit Stop, trying to get enough drinks in me to forget how you *ruined my fucking life*—and who do I see sitting just a few tables away? *Who do I see?*"

"Please, man...I'm sorry. I just—"

"Shut the fuck up!"

Lydia cannot remember ever being more afraid; not even during those terrible moments pinned against the telephone pole. But as great as this fear is, it is secondary next to the revelation that has suddenly been placed before her: her father is close. Closer than he's ever been. Close enough to touch.

She can finally reach out to him in the same way she has done for Gregory. Gain insight into his anger, his sorrow. And perhaps find a way to help him.

Unseen by the two men, Lydia walks between them and places a small, pale hand over her father's wrist. The memory she receives is alarmingly vivid, and—

—more than he can possibly take. He just can't believe the fucking *nerve* of this guy. That bastard should have withered away behind bars for the entirety of his ten-year sentence—the courts owed him that much justice, Chuck thinks. But no, the skinny little weasel was out in less than five (for *good behavior*, they say)—and now here he is, just a few tables away. Pouting to himself, of all things. Feeling sorry for himself. Pouting about how the job market's hard with a criminal rap sheet, or how he has to give a plastic box a blow job every time he wants to start his car—some stupid shit like that.

And how is he coping with his insignificant woes? By getting drunk enough to spill himself behind the wheel of another car and kill another little girl when he forgets to turn his lights on. The asshole only thinks of himself; there's no consideration for those he's hurt, those he's *ruined*. The skinny little weasel doesn't know what it's like to watch your marriage crumble once you and your wife are no longer able to glance at one another without seeing what has been lost. How it hurts to see strangers living in the home you once shared with your family.

He can't fathom the agony of identifying your daughter's broken body for the county medical examiner, or how strong the temptation can be to jump into the open grave with her as the casket is being lowered into the—

—cold solace of night. She has retreated into the darkness, as far away from the glaring headlights and her father as she can get. As far away as the invisible cell of her memorial will allow. What Lydia has seen—*felt*—has frightened her beyond measure. So much anger. So much pain.

"You're not going anywhere, asshole."

"Please...I know it was a mistake to come into town. A really big mistake, and I'm sorry."

"I don't give a single shit about your apologies, either. Way I see it, I've got nothing else to hang around for, and you sure as hell don't, either." The gun in Charles Mitchell's hand ceases its wild wavering.

"No! Please God, please God, please God—"

Lydia wants to steer clear of this runaway series of events, but she can't. Both men are here because of her. Charles Mitchell is about to do something he will never be able to take back—much like Greg did—and she *won't* watch it happen. So, she takes a gamble, moves forward, and touches him again.

As it had been with Gregory, this second touch not only receives memories, but also channels them. However, these channeled memories are not her father's. They are her own.

She sends them out in fragments, brief camera flashes. They are all from the perspective of her lonely roadside memorial. Small windows into her time spent with a penitent man.

He sits cross-legged in the grass before her planted cross. By flashlight, he reads from the daily journal he kept in prison. A chronicle of every wrong he can remember ever committing under the influence of alcohol, and how he intends for such wrongs to never happen again.

He paces excitedly among the floral arrangements, breathlessly relating to her that after seven years' sobriety, his ex-wife Cynthia has finally agreed to talk. He's one careful step closer to seeing his daughter.

He slumps before the planted cross, head in his hands. Seeing Kayla seems no longer a possibility—and perhaps it's for the best. He is dead to her, after all.

As Lydia feeds these fragments to her father (along with many others, rapid-fire), she continues to receive as well. Charles Mitchell's thoughts are still heavy with anger and pain, but other feelings are beginning to dilute the mixture. A generous dose of confusion. A few drops of sadness. And...the slightest pinch of empathy.

Lydia watches as her father's extended arm lowers slightly. His grip on the gun loosens. In turn, she loosens her own grip, then lets go.

"I swear to God, you'll never see me again, Mr. Mitchell," Greg stammers, his voice practically vibrating with fear. "Just let me walk away and—" Greg swallows the rest of his plea with a gasp of surprise.

Charles has dropped his gun. He makes a tearful glance toward the planted cross—and his unseen daughter, who stands beside it—and falls to the ground in turn. He turtles himself upon the yellowed grass, knees and elbows brought together, head tucked into his chest. His cracked human shell begins to shudder with silent sobs, and eventually erupts in a gargled, anguished moan. "Please tell me you're home now, Honey Bear. Please...tell me you're home..."

The night is silent save for the hum of the car engine and the rhythmic chirp of cicadas. Lydia speaks into the stillness with the first words that come to mind.

"I'm home, Daddy. As long as you and Greg are with me, I'll...always be home."

To Lydia's surprise, her father's sobs taper off like water from a closed faucet. His hitching shoulders settle. It's almost as if he's heard her.

A shadow flickers before the headlights' glare. It is Gregory.

Though the barrel of a gun no longer holds him captive, he does not flee. Instead, he slowly inches toward the man who nearly shot him. When he is close enough, he lowers himself to the ground. Extends a pale hand shakily toward Charles.

Lydia watches as her father tenses at the touch; reflexively, she does the same. The shell Charles's body has constructed for itself begins to loosen and eventually goes slack as the broken man sits up. Cast in the revealing glare of headlights, the two men meet eye to eye.

"I'm so sorry for taking her away from you," Greg says. "So goddamn sorry."

It happens as each man continues to stare into the eyes—the *soul*—of the other. It is a brief but fiery spark that ignites within their hearts—the beginning of something truly transformative between them. Something that may herald an eventual under-standing.

Reconciliation. Closure.

This spark also fills Lydia with a warmth that blossoms to encompass her entirely. Within its embrace, she watches as the glare of headlights gives way to a light more intense than the brightest rays of the sun. It illuminates County Road 117 in a way she has never seen before. It is no longer a lonely macadam ribbon stretching endlessly into the murky fog of death. It is no longer a road leading nowhere.

Instead, Lydia thinks it might just lead her home.

Andy Coe lives in northern Colorado with his spoiled cat. By day he is a software engineer, but by night he spends his hours writing horror. He has published both short- and long-form fiction on Kindle Vella and is currently working toward the publication of his first full-length novel.

You Can't Stay Here

Kevin Higgins

"Not to be occupied and not to exist are one and the same thing for a man."
– Voltaire

It took me a bit to process what had happened after I woke up in my garage.

Well, not "woke up."

Not exactly.

For starters, I could see my body there on the poured concrete, blood oozing from the hole in my head where, moments before, my neighbor had bashed my brains in with a hammer.

My own hammer, actually.

From my own toolbox.

Is that considered irony?

You can probably tell I'm no writer. Furthest from, actually—I am (was?) a CPA. I'm a numbers guy. But I'm also the only guy I know who's found himself standing over his own corpse, so I figure that buys me a little narrative grace.

Twenty seconds in and I'm already digressing.

Let me try to explain.

Human me was dead, okay? From where I stood, I could see that clear as day.

In fact, I suddenly found that I could see everything with amazing clarity. The giant cavity in the side of my head, for one. The growing pool of blood beneath it, still spreading across the floor, redirected this way and that by all the clutter (Susan was always on me to clean up the garage, *it's not safe for the kids*, all of that). And the hammer, the instrument of my demise, half under the shelving unit where we kept the Christmas decorations, right where that dickhead Whitlock had tossed it when he decided that I wasn't going to get any deader.

How could I see these things, you ask?

Well, that's the thing.

I was dead. But I also wasn't.

I'm not sure how else to put this, but as far as I could tell, there were two of me: Very Dead Me sprawled out on the floor, and Not Quite Dead Me (the *me* that's telling this story) standing over him.

It was nothing like the movies, I'll tell you that right up front. Whatever ghostly image you have in your head, forget it. I wasn't translucent or floating or anything like that. I was very much *there*.

As I brushed myself off (like I said, the garage was filthy), I could see my hands, my body, my feet. I could feel the watch on my wrist, the knotty stitching of my blue cable knit sweater (a birthday gift from the kids), the stickiness of the bald patches in my old fuzzy moccasins (my "shuffling shoes", as I liked to call them). It was like a spontaneous cloning had occurred, like Not

Quite Dead Me had molted out of Very Dead Me, or some other scientific term I've long forgotten for when one becomes two.

I realize that what I'm describing probably sounds ridiculous. Believe me, I know. Before I get too far into this, I just want to say that I'm not a religious man. I've never believed in the afterlife. I'm pretty sure God doesn't exist; if he did, I doubt he'd co-sign my asshole neighbor caving in my skull over a dispute about a dead tree.

Honestly, when it comes to death, I'd always envisioned something much simpler:

When you die, you're dead.

Back to the earth. Worm food. That's it.

So as you might imagine, I was feeling pretty foolish, standing there in a pool of my own blood. Because I *did* die, and yet here I was, just hanging around the crime scene, like some sort of post-mortem insurance adjuster.

One of the first things I noticed was that I seemed to have all of my senses. Like I told you already, I could see everything; I've already described the sorry state of my dead body (a little bit anyway, I'll spare you the details). I could smell, too: the cloying musk of Whitlock's drugstore aftershave lingered in the air, the particles or atoms or whatever still in motion from when he drove the claw end of the hammer deep into my skull. And I could hear just fine, because I heard quite clearly when Susan returned from her book club, the all-weather tires I had recently put on her Subaru crunching down the gravel driveway, stopping just outside the garage.

Right away I had some questions:

Could I speak?

Could I be seen by others?

Could I pass through walls? (Okay, that one was more wishful thinking.)

To test the first, I immediately started screaming at the top of my lungs, "*Help!*" and "*Susan!*" and maybe a couple other things I'd rather not write down. The garage door was closed, though I could swear it was open earlier (that's how Whitlock came in to confront me—he must have closed it on his way out). On the other side of it, I heard the car door open, then close, then the sound of Susan's footsteps fading toward the house. If she could hear me, she would've heard me, I'll just say that; but there was no urgency in her gait, so I was pretty sure right then and there that my human voice (at least as a means of communication with the living) was gone.

While I waited for Susan to get inside, I ran another inventory. I touched the side of my head, right above my left ear, where Whitlock had done his business with the hammer. The hole was there, and the blood too, an exact match to the *me* lying at my feet. I ran my index and middle finger around the edges of the wound, feeling its rubbery jaggedness, folding and squeezing the rips and flaps of tattered flesh.

I gritted my teeth, ready to scream in agony, but there was no sensation at all.

To say this was bizarre would be an understatement. You don't realize how alive your skin is—how finely attuned to touch, to temperature, to stimuli of all kinds—until you can no longer feel anything.

I'm not proud of what I did next, but I wanted to make sure. I walked (not floated) over to my workbench, grabbed the screwdriver that I had been using earlier in the day to fix the seat on Danny's bike, and without thinking much, plunged it into the back of my left hand. I winced as it entered, prepared for the rush of agony to follow, but there was none.

I lifted my hand and pushed the rest of the screwdriver clean through to the other side, breaking the meaty skin on my palm.

I wiggled it, twisted it, moved it back and forth.

Still nothing.

No pain, no blood.

It was like all the fragilities of my physical form had turned off at the point of expiration, like they had all died with the guy that lay there on that filthy floor. I still had a body, but not really; it appeared to be disposable, a shell, a means of movement and sensory intake and not much more. What seemed to have survived most prominently in this post-hammer version of myself were the things that made me who I am: my thoughts, my memories, my disturbing knowledge of the US tax code.

I'm going to pause here for a second. For those keeping score at home, that's sight, sound and smell, yes; pain, blood and injury, no.

If that sounds cool, I can assure you it's not.

This wasn't some drunken wish granted by a monkey's paw. I was impervious to pain because I was *dead*. And eventually Susan (or God forbid, Danny or Joyce) was going to head out to the garage and find Very Dead Me on the floor, drenched in my own gore, a deep, ugly crater in the side of my head. I could picture every painful moment. They would fall to their knees, clutch their head, claw at their eyes. There would be many questions but few answers. They would have sleepless night after sleepless night, for who knows how long. They would probably never be the same.

I'm not ashamed to admit that it was around this time that I had a mini breakdown. I felt it rise up from deep within, my mind suddenly flush with sharp, quick flashes of light and dark. I braced myself on the workbench; there was nothing I could do except stand there and take it.

For the tough guys out there, I'll just say this: spend some time in purgatory and then get back to me. Because that's what this was; suddenly I was sure of it. Purgatory. The waiting room for the afterlife. The place where souls went when they still had *shit to do* before reaching their final resting place.

Now the questions came fast and furious:

What the hell was I still doing here?

What was the point of all this?

What shit was left for me to do?

When the flashes passed, I pulled the screwdriver out of my hand and placed it back on the workbench, careful to do so quietly. I didn't know for sure, but it felt like a safe assumption that even if my voice couldn't be heard by the living, any object that I interacted with was still fair game for the usual rules of the universe.

By now I could hear Susan in the house, moving around, getting ready to veg out with her backlog of soaps on the DVR. There was little chance she would come into the garage tonight. Which, I have to say, was a relief. Same for the kids; Danny was staying the night at a friend's, and Joyce was probably in her room, nose in a book (I swear, I don't know what I did to deserve that one—she's going to be something someday).

That bought me some time.

I found the pile of folded tarps behind the lawnmower, grabbed the largest one, and draped it carefully over my body. Not a permanent solution, but it at least granted Very Dead Me some temporary modesty.

Very quietly, I opened the inner garage door and stepped into the laundry room. The room was dark, and the machines were quiet; Susan had just done a wash earlier. I could see Joyce's softball jersey air-drying on the rack.

Would I ever see her play again?

It was too sad to think about.

From the small space, I could hear the TV, the hyper-affected prattle of some pitchman selling dryer sheets. That meant that Susan was in the kitchen, probably making tea. She had this thing where she liked to use the TV as background noise. A waste of electricity, if you ask me, but in marriage you pick your battles.

I left the laundry room for the main hallway that separated the bedrooms from the kitchen and living room. From the opposite end of the darkened hall, I could hear the faint drift of music, some pop singer who Joyce kept begging me to take her to see. Another wave of sadness hit when I realized that day would never come.

I followed the music to Joyce's bedroom. Through the crack of the door, I could see her cross-legged on the bed, textbook open, papers scattered everywhere. She was gnawing at the end of a pen (a habit I had when I was her age), studying her notes, lost in thought.

I leaned in a little closer to see if I could make out the subject, and in doing so, inadvertently pushed the door open with my big, dumb head. The old hinges screamed under the weight of the heavy oak slab, a neck-tensing, high-pitched *CCRREEAAKK*.

Before I could duck back into the dark, Joyce whipped her head around, following the sound.

I froze in the doorframe.

"Who's there?" Joyce's voice. My little Joyce.

For some dumb reason, I closed my eyes.

A moment passed, then two.

Slowly, I opened them again. Joyce was staring right at me.

No, not at me.

Through me.

I looked my daughter square in the face, the face I had seen day after day, week after week, month after month, eleven years running.

I can't say we locked eyes, because we didn't.

She had no idea I was there.

For what felt like forever, neither of us moved. I dared not speak, though I knew she wouldn't hear me if I did. I dared not move, either; the last thing I wanted to do was make more noise.

After an overlong stalemate, Joyce finally rose from the bed.

She took one step in my direction.

Another.

Then she turned, heading instead to the window, which she closed and locked. I swung out of the doorframe and leaned against the cool of the hallway wall.

Invisible.

To my own child.

I wish it on nobody.

I waited in the hall until I heard the groan of bedsprings. When I was sure that Joyce had returned to her studies, I tiptoed back in the direction of the living room. Susan was on the couch now, the top of her head barely visible above the overstuffed cushions. On the television, a young blonde woman begged an older gentleman not to leave.

When the woman on TV began shouting, I scurried into the foyer, suddenly grateful for the carpet Susan had insisted on installing when we moved in.

As quietly as I could, I opened the front door and stepped into the cool autumn air. I had to get out, to regroup. My own home had become a museum, a collection of things I could look at but no longer possess. It was overwhelmingly upsetting.

To the west, the last remnants of sun streaked the horizon a rich orange. To the east (where Whitlock lived), deep bands of blue and purple pulled across the sky, escorting the night that would soon follow. I stood there for a moment, trying to appreciate what I might never get to experience again. Or might experience over and over again, ad infinitum. Both options felt equally defeating.

Through the breezy sway of the trees along the property line, I could see a single light on in Whitlock's house.

First floor, back room.

His den.

I knew the room well. On summer evenings, when the bastard's windows were open, I could often hear him yelling at the screen, berating Yankee after Yankee for swinging at garbage. His cigar smoke would drift up and out, hanging over us like a pall, reminding us of his odious presence.

It was autumn now, and the windows were closed, but the Yanks were still in it, so I was pretty sure that I knew where Whitlock was.

And then it came to me, as close to a divine vision as I'll ever admit to having. As I stood there in the blue-purple wane of that October night, the side of my head split open wide enough for birds to nest, a singular thought took root in my mind:

I'm going to get that motherfucker back.

It wasn't any more complicated than that. Suddenly, I just knew. *That* was why I was still here, wandering around with a hole in my head.

Revenge, pure and simple.

From the day Susan and I had moved onto the block, Whitlock was a prick. I remember seeing him at the edge of his lawn, holding a pickaxe, glowering at Danny and Joyce as they ran around the yard, exploring their new space. When I went over to introduce myself, he wouldn't shake my hand, instead reminding me to keep "those little fuckers" out of his garden.

He was an awful guy, through and through. Rude, prickly, quick to offend and take offense. Fortunately, he spent most of his time inside, doing God knows what. Every once in a while, while raking the leaves or mowing the grass, I would see him outside, planting this or that (for a miserable piece of shit, the guy sure liked his flowers). On occasion, our eyes would lock, an unfortunate consequence of poor timing on his part or mine. When they did, I could feel the hate flowing through him—for me, for my family, for our outward displays of happiness and contentment.

And then today. As I tried to recall the incident in the garage, I found that I could only remember small flashes, like a storm several miles off the coast.

The downed limb.

The argument.

The way his spittle hung in the air as he swung the hammer.

Then blackness.

I know I told you earlier that I couldn't float. But let me tell you something: I damn near floated over to Whitlock's property. Every step felt like a triumph, every push forward an orgasm. For the first time since becoming whatever *this* was, I was armed with knowledge and purpose.

I knew what I had to do.

And boy, was I excited to do it.

I crossed the property line at a small gap in the hydrangea, stepping directly over the tree limb we had bickered about hours earlier (I don't care what that asshole says—the ordinance is very clear). As expected, Whitlock's yard was empty, save for two squirrels chasing each other through the massive flower beds that flanked both sides of his front door.

The first thing I did was stomp the hell out of his goldenrod. I want to say I'm not proud of it, but fuck that. It was great fun. The chrysanthemums were next, followed by the snapdragon and sunflowers. When my moccasins became clumped and heavy with soil, I kicked them off, using my bare heel to grind the remaining pansies into pulp. Then I bent down and began ripping them out by the root, two at a time, working with a healthy mix of precision and glee.

When I was done in the flower beds, I climbed the three steps to the front door and tried the handle. To my surprise, it was unlocked. I slipped inside, closing the door quietly behind me.

For the first few moments, I did nothing but stand in the small, dim foyer and take in my surroundings. Not that it was some great bucket list item or anything, but I had never actually been in Whitlock's house.

What I saw was horrifying.

There was stuff everywhere, garbage and knickknacks and boxes filled to the brim with assorted crap. Directly in front of me, a carpeted staircase led upward to darkness, the sides of each step piled high with trash. To my left, in what must have once been the dining room, every inch of the dark oak table was covered with junk, wholly unsuitable for guests or a meal. And to my right, the narrow hall that presumably led to the back of the house was lined with stacks upon stacks of papers and magazines, some toppled over.

From where I stood, I could hear the faint, even warble of John Sterling describing the nuanced differences between a two-seam and four-seam fastball. The door at the end of the hall was closed, but I could see a scant sliver of light above the jamb, the colors flickering and changing with the images on the screen.

All of the sudden, a sort of analysis paralysis set in.

I had to make this count.

Acting purely on instinct, I opened the front door a crack, leaned out to press the doorbell, then ducked into the darkness of the dining room, careful not to disturb any of the mess. From somewhere in the house, a faint series of chimed notes rang out a simple melody.

I stood in the shadows and waited. I was worried that Whitlock wouldn't hear the bell with the TV on, but after a minute, I saw the far wall of the hallway brighten as somebody opened the door at the other end. And then I heard him, shambling down the hallway, muttering something under his breath.

At last he appeared in the foyer, his hair wet from a recent shower, wearing sweat shorts and an oversized promotional tee from the local supermarket. In the thin backlight from the hallway, he looked smaller, older, weaker. I wondered where he'd stashed the clothes he was wearing when he killed me—there's no way those things weren't gross.

He paused in the middle of the room, still a few feet from the door. Now I could see a gun in his far hand, held down by his leg in an unsteady grip.

"Who is it?" he barked in the direction of the door.

"It's me, asshole," I whispered, knowing he couldn't hear me. I suddenly felt recharged, invincible.

When nobody answered, Whitlock took a step closer to the door, raising the gun slightly. Then he yanked it open, as if trying to get the jump on whoever was on the other side. I don't know who he was expecting—maybe Susan, maybe Danny, maybe the police—but he was immediately disappointed to find the porch free and clear.

I waited with a smile, knowing what would happen next.

"My fucking flowers! My goddamn garden!"

There it was.

Then he disappeared outside. I couldn't see him, but I could imagine him out there, spinning wildly in all directions, waving his gun around, looking for something to shoot.

While he was gone, I slipped out of the dining room and down the hallway, into his den. It was even filthier than the front of the house. Empty beer bottles covered most of the floor. There were dirty plates on every conceivable surface, some molding over, some carrying the nubs of spent cigars. The only clear surface was an old recliner in the center of the room, its arms a patchwork of stains. On the TV, the Yanks were down 5-3.

I sat down in the recliner and waited.

Five minutes passed, then ten. I knew Whitlock was outside somewhere, stalking the yard, looking for the person who had destroyed his garden.

That was fine. I could wait.

I had all the time in the world.

Then I heard the front door close, followed by the climb of heavy feet.

Whitlock was upstairs now.

I considered following him, but decided to stay put. He would be back. He was nothing if not a creature of habit.

I watched as the Yankees rallied to load the bases. Too bad Whitlock was missing this.

Finally I heard him again, lumbering back down the stairs. His footsteps were thicker now, angrier. I heard something topple over in the hallway, heard him kick it in frustration. I kept my eyes locked on the television, not wanting to rock the chair, to make a sound.

And then he stopped. Exactly where, I wasn't sure. From where I was sitting, I still couldn't see him. The sound of the game faded as I listened intently.

Did he sense something wrong?

Did he know I was there?

Then all at once he came around the chair, still holding the gun, a fresh beer in his other hand. His gaze was affixed on the TV, where the Orioles were swapping pitchers.

Right in front of me now. I could feel the heat from his body, could smell the off-putting stink of his aftershave, a smell I would forever associate with the swing of that hammer.

He wasn't looking at the chair as he sat in my lap.

I felt his body tense instantly with shock as he realized that someone—*something*—was in his recliner with him.

I did the only thing I could think to do in the moment.

I blew in his ear.

Immediately, Whitlock launched himself up and out. He scrambled backward and fell, unable to find purchase atop the empties that littered the floor, sending his gun and beer flying in opposite directions.

I rose slowly, not in any real rush. I made a point to rock the chair, to kick some bottles, to make my presence known. He couldn't see me, but he could damn sure hear me. I saw his eyes widen in disbelief, his head whip erratically back and forth like a lawn sprinkler set to high, looking for something, anything, seeing nothing.

When he tried to stand, I pushed him backward, watched him tumble into a pile of old newspapers.

I'm not a violent guy by nature. Never was. Susan used to call me her "big sweaty teddy." But now, because of the insufferable scumbag in front of me, she would never be able to call me that again.

Whitlock had taken everything from me. My life. My future. My family. And still—I didn't pick up the gun. I grabbed the open beer instead, still three quarters full. I lifted it over my head and poured, letting the foamy liquid cascade down over my head and shoulders. I knew Whitlock could see it all, could see the figure of a man taking shape as the liquid outlined the contours of my body. I knew I was breaking his weak little mind.

He pitched forward, eyes bulging. I saw his neck muscles seize, the veins thick and red.

And then he was gone.

I watched the life leave his eyes as his heart gave out. That's another thing that's not like it is on TV, by the way. He didn't clutch at his chest, grab his left arm, moan in agony. He was alive, and then he was dead. That was it.

I shook him to make sure. When his head lolled heavily to the side, I knew. It was over.

Back in the Bronx, the Yanks went down swinging.

I walked back down the hallway, through the dining room and into the kitchen, where I found the cordless handset for Whitlock's landline atop a pile of counter clutter. I checked for a dial tone, dialed 911, then placed it in the sink to ring.

When I left through the front door, I didn't bother to close it.

Standing on Whitlock's stoop, I noticed it for the first time. At first I thought it was a trick of the light, fading as it was in the evening's rapid march toward night. But holding my hands up to the bulb of the porch lamp only confirmed it:

I was fading away.

I looked down at my arms, my legs, my feet. It was happening everywhere, and rather quickly, the color and depth draining from torso and limb alike. All at once I remembered the fantastic crêpes from the corner *boulangerie* that Susan and I had devoured for breakfast each morning during our honeymoon in Paris. How delicate, how paper-thin they were.

How fragile.

That was me now.

It was almost closing time.

You don't have to go home, but you can't stay here.

Well, I did go home. Across the yard, through the bushes, back inside. Part of me hoped that I would find Susan in a tizzy, frantically calling friends and family to inquire about my whereabouts, to ask if they'd heard from me. Instead I found her right where I'd left her, on the right side of the couch, watching her program. Her eyelids looked heavier, sleepier. I moved carefully past her into the hall, down to Joyce's room. Through the crack in her door, I could see Joyce asleep now, textbook in her lap. I remembered her telling me earlier that she had a big test tomorrow.

I hope she did well.

I'm back in my office now (really just a walk-in closet we converted during the pandemic so that I could work from home). When I'm done telling my story (and I'm almost done, I promise), I'll leave this laptop on, with this document open. Someone will find it soon enough; maybe Susan, maybe the police when they finally come, but probably Danny (he's always on my computer messing around).

If someone from my family finds this first, don't look under the tarp in the garage—just call the police. You don't want to remember me that way.

And to Danny and Joyce: as much as I want you to grow up believing that revenge is never the answer, I can't deny that sometimes it is. I'm proof of that.

I'm almost gone now. I can barely see my hands as they type this. Which puts me in the weird position of having to wrap this up before the end.

Not the hammer-to-the-head end I experienced a couple hours ago. The *real* end.

I don't want to spend my final moments at this keyboard, where I've wasted so many hours reading IRS memos, crunching numbers, carrying the one. We spend the bulk of our lives doing useless things in the service of a paycheck, things we bend over backward to convince ourselves of just how important they are.

They're not, by the way.

I'm going to sign off here. If you think I'm leaving you with a cliffhanger, think again—I know better than that. As far I know, there's no sequel coming—this story is one-and-done.

That doesn't mean I'm leaving without questions. I have only one, actually:

What happens next?

I guess I'm okay with not knowing.

We're not meant to have all the answers.

That's what makes us human.

From the living room, I can hear the mindless din of the nightly news, the over-serious anchor gravely describing the scene of a four-alarm fire a few towns away. More death, more tragedy. Just another day on Earth.

That means Susan fell asleep on the couch again. I think I'll go sit with her one last time, until I fade away completely.

And on the off chance that Whitlock is now wandering around in the ether like I just was, and on the off chance that he somehow reads this:

That tree limb was your responsibility, not mine.

Kevin Higgins lives in New Jersey, where he enjoys hanging out with his wife and daughter, listening to punk rock and watching reruns of *King of Queens*. A video producer by trade, Kevin picked up writing in his thirties, focusing on horror and thriller short fiction. His stories have been published by Undertaker Books and Terrorcore Publishing. His favorite author is Richard Chizmar.

CHARON SWIMS

CHRISTOPHER O'HALLORAN

Styx, Gjöll, Hitfun, Hubur, Sanzu.

There are many names for it, but Charon has achieved an intimacy that transcends names. He thinks of it as *his river*, across which he ferries the dead.

The dead who pay, that is.

His back is weary and his mind is frayed. It's been a long day.

It's been a long eternity.

The dead come with baggage on baggage. Sorrow and pain. They come fleeing such feelings and don't realize they can leave it all on earth.

Or at least most don't. His current passenger defies the norm. His hands are clasped in his lap. His back is straight. His head swivels, taking in the sights: the shore, the ink-black waters, the sturdy wood beneath him, keeping him safe.

"Do you row all day, old timer?"

Old timer? The man in Charon's punt doesn't look much younger than him. Sure, his skin isn't paper thin and grey like Charon's, but the passenger has his fair share of wrinkles. Hair more white than black. His posture isn't stooped, but maybe he's putting on airs for Charon. Maybe he's putting everything he has in keeping his spine ramrod straight.

"I take ten minutes on the other side," says Charon. "Little breaks."

The dead don't usually speak to him. They lament the whole ferry ride. Can never just enjoy the moment. Watch the occasional ripple on the surface of the river. Imagine what's beneath while taking solace in the fact that they'll never know.

Even Charon doesn't know. He'll keep it that way, thank you very much.

"Is the other side as enjoyable as I've led my congregation to believe?"

"You'll find out soon enough."

The man in Charon's punt nods solemnly.

Truth be told, Charon doesn't know. Not half as much as he'd like. He rests on the other side, sure, but they don't let him wander. They don't let him rejoice in the fruits of the afterlife.

Charon and his passenger are still close enough to the river's edge to hear the wailing of the cheapskates left behind. More who will never know heavenly joy.

Is it so hard to die with a little metal in your pocket? You don't need to place coins on your eyes; Charon's a modern man. Just yesterday he accepted a dented Zippo from a fellow who stepped in front of a semi-truck. Easy.

The payment, that is. The death sounded like a troubled affair of laboured breathing, lost fluids, and intestines spilled on dusty asphalt.

"Do you ever pity the poor?" asks the man in Charon's punt.

Charon glances down at the guy.

Of course. He's wearing a priest's collar. Full up on that Catholic guilt and eager to share it with the rest of the class.

"Keep the judgement to yourself, father," says Charon, lifting his eyes. "I don't need it. I've been doing this longer than you can imagine."

"What use have you for coin? I wouldn't think there'd be a 7-11 in Hell. A Tommy Bahama hidden behind Cerberus."

Charon smirks. "Usually the ones making that argument are the ones being left behind. Not those who've boarded."

"You get many men of the cloth in your canoe?"

The priest scooches closer. Shifting seats to attain some sort of religious fulfilment in chatting with such a pivotal figurehead in the underworld as Charon.

"Punt. Not a canoe."

"Sorry," says the priest. "Your punt."

Charon shrugs. "I get enough. Few so talkative."

"I find that hard to believe."

A hand emerges from the water, gnarled fingers grasping for help.

Charon pushes it back under with his pole.

"Believe it," he says. "They either clam right up or start speaking in tongues. Few expect this. Pearly gates, this is not."

"No," says the priest. "I can't imagine my brothers embracing this version of the afterlife."

"Not a problem for you, father?" Charon doesn't know why he's engaging. He should just shut his mouth and push onward. Like he always has, like he always will.

But it's been a long day. He needs something to take his thoughts off the glass under his shoulder blades. The weakness in his knees.

"I've always maintained...differing beliefs. Kept an open mind."

"You're not like the other priests."

"No," says the priest, the mockery either ignored or going over his head. "I was an exorcist."

"You don't say." Charon's pole sticks in something. He yanks and yanks until whatever filth has grasped onto it releases its hold. For good measure, he gives the creature a jab with the pole before shoving onward.

The priest observes the shore they left behind, crammed full of souls doomed to wander purgatory penniless.

"My Church distanced itself from the process long ago, despite what the public has been led to believe by movies. But I..." He shakes his head. "I couldn't stand by when my flock needed help."

"I bet those demons were shaking in their hooves."

"Joke all you want, but at least *I* helped."

"Ouch."

The priest falls silent.

Charon pushes on. It's not like him to pity his charges, but something about this day feels different. He's spoken more during this trip than any other in memory, and his memory is aeons long. Aeons of work. Charon is tired.

"Might I try a push?" asks the priest.

The audacity. The sheer entitlement. This man thinks he has the ability to navigate these treacherous waters?

"Be my guest." Charon holds the pole out to the priest and steps down into the sitting area of the punt.

With a nod and a smile, the priest climbs to the pushing position.

Charon doesn't know why he relinquished control over the most important vessel in the underworld. A small part of his brain is going feral. Panic demands he take over immediately, but his bone-deep weariness smothers the panic like a flame.

"How many souls have you freed?" asks Charon. "How many devils have you banished back to Hell?"

The priest clicks his tongue. "Far too many to count. But I don't banish them back to Hell. They might return." He navigates the river well, much as Charon hates to admit it. The priest pushes the punt through the water as if he's been doing it all his life.

"You can't *destroy* a demon." Charon wants to laugh at the possibility. "What do you do, stick them in a corked bottle? Take them within yourself? Have you Legion in your bowels?"

The priest smiles down at Charon. "You are on the right track. My body is excellent at filtering out the possessions."

"You're shitting me."

The priest gives Charon a knowing glance while pushing off the bed of the river.

"Like I said," he says, "you're on the right track. I'd imagine there's many a sewage system possessed by angry entities."

Charon's mouth falls open. And he'd thought he'd seen it all. "Hades help us if one latches onto a gator under New York."

They drift slightly. Maybe the priest isn't as capable as Charon thought. He'll let the man struggle. Make him ask for help.

Humble him.

At this rate they'll never reach the other side. At this rate, they'll sooner reach the point where they began the crossing. Back to those whiners and their grubby mitts. Their pleas for help.

Charon doesn't care. He hasn't for a long, long time. Eternity does that to a man.

"Tell me of your vocation," says Charon. "I hear so little about above."

"Do you want to hear about my experiences or do you want to hear about the average life, because they are not one in the same."

"If I wanted the news, I'd pick up a paper."

"They have papers in the underworld?"

Charon groans. "You have no sense of humour."

"I'm surprised you do."

Infinite lifetimes stuck in this dredge, you need humour. Charon flicks his hand at the priest.

"Tell me about the life of a modern-day exorcist."

The priest lets the pole drift behind the boat and wipes sweat from his brow.

"I don't enjoy dwelling on those in dire straits."

"And yet, you'll needle me on leaving behind a few souls?" Charon scoffs. "If I'm going to be forced to think about it, you are too."

The priest thinks on it. "I'll tell you one instance. But this is confidential."

"Who am I going to tell?"

"Fair enough." The priest looks into the distance as if seeing his life projected before him. "There was a boy. Thirteen. His name was Jeremy, but friends called him 'Jare'. He had a lot of friends. Or at least he did before the possession.

"The demon that possessed him had no name. Usually, identifying the entity would give me enough of a hold to suck them from the possessed, so as you could imagine, I had my work cut out for me."

"How did you know he was possessed?" Charon asks. "Spinning head?"

The priest smiles. "He was visiting adult websites. Being rude to girls in his class. Skipping school and even..." He looks from left to right, slowly. Scanning the water for eavesdroppers. "Smoking marijuana."

"That's just a teen."

"He also ritualistically slaughtered the family dog and slept on the ceiling."

"That's a little rarer."

"That was Jare." The priest pushes them along. "Where was I?"

"Through the desert on an imp with no name."

"Yes," says the priest. "The name." He smiles. "I needed another way in. I considered what drew the demon to the boy. The attitudes. The characteristics. I wondered how I could emulate them and make myself an attractive alternative."

"You pretended to be a teen boy?"

"I did. I put on a carefree affect while mentioning the influence—exaggerated, of course—I had among my parish. I feigned bravado. Ignorance. I spoke to the demon as if I was a fool.

"It fell for it. It slid inside me, hoping to use my ignorance to manipulate me into causing havoc within the church."

"And you turned it into waste."

"Two days later while doing the *New York Times* crossword."

Charon rests his chin on his knuckles. "Fascinating."

The priest looks down at Charon. His passenger. "There's a benefit to the soul, when you help another."

"That sentiment doesn't count for shit down here, father. The game has already been played. The score is already tallied."

"So, kindness doesn't exist down here?"

Charon shrugs. "Shouldn't."

"Because it doesn't get you a reward?"

"Precisely."

The priest shakes his head. Is that disgust on his face? No, a man so pious would never stoop so low.

Still...

"What dwells in these waters, old timer?"

There it is again. *Old timer*.

"You're no spring chicken yourself, father."

"Does the term offend you?"

"No. I'm beyond offence." Charon looks forward. Yes, they're definitely going in the wrong direction now. He'd hoped for more of a reprieve, but there's a reason why he's the master of this river. "It's time for me to take the pole again."

The priest says nothing. He continues pushing.

"Now who's the old timer," mutters Charon as he struggles to his feet. "Can't even hear me."

"You didn't tell me what's in the water," says the priest. "Something is trying to slow us down."

"Yes," says Charon. "You." Unsteadily, he reaches out a hand for the pole.

The priest starts to lift the pole out of the water. His eyes flick over Charon's shoulder.

Charon doesn't like that look. He turns.

There is the shore. A miserable crowd milling about.

A teenaged boy—maybe the same age as Jeremy, Jare to his friends—takes a step into the dark water. Another. He's only knee deep when something pulls his legs out from under him.

He disappears before he has the chance to scream.

He's going back for them. Knowing strikes Charon a fleeting instant before the pole does.

Unlike the teen, he does have time to scream.

The force of the priest's shove pushes Charon backward. The gunwale of the punt comes up to his knees and forces the collapse of his legs. His ass falls over the edge, but he holds onto the gunwale with gnarled fingers.

It's a humiliating image. The wood of the punt digging into the back of his knees; his hands scrabbling for purchase.

The water laps at his rear end. It's not frigid like he expected. It's warm. A comforting caress.

It's a trap.

"Help," he cries. "Father!"

The priest stands over him, pole in hand.

"You sound like them. The penniless."

"Have mercy." Charon hates the whine in his voice. It lacks the dignity of his position.

"I do," says the priest. "That's why I must do this."

The pole goes hard into Charon's chest. He sinks farther but holds on fast.

The priest rears back and strikes again, but this time on Charon's fingers.

Charon cries out. Agony lances through his bones. Never have they felt so old!

"Stop!"

The other hand, now. He can't hang on.

The priest brings the pole down like an axe.

Yelping, Charon falls back. His legs hold on, but the water engulfs his head and chest as he hangs backward.

Don't look, don't look. He wouldn't be able to unsee. To un-know.

Hands on his feet. Around his ankles.

The priest has changed his mind. He'll pull Charon in. Of course he will. Since Charon was given this posting, no one has dared attack him. This was just a blip. A test of his weariness. Failure doesn't mean termination. It's a wake-up call not to drop your guard. No matter how weary this existence has made him.

The priest lifts Charon's legs and dumps him into his river.

Charon sinks into the warmth. It whispers to him.

Open your eyes. Open your mouth. Breathe me in.

It's a refrain he's gotten used to tuning out, but tumbling under the surface, the whisper is loud as a train whistle.

Charon swims, but with his eyes closed, there's no way of knowing if he's swimming up or down.

He stops moving. Just a quick glance, that's all he needs. Just enough to orient himself. His lungs scream for oxygen, but if he swims down instead of up, they'll get nothing.

Just one look. The light of the surface, or the darkness of the deep.

Charon opens his eyes.

A crowd of hairless, smiling faces peer up at him like curious children. The river has smoothed all features of their faces, made grotesque pebbles of their heads. Their eyes are pale, covered in a ghostly film. They enjoy being observed; their mouths open even wider as thin lips form his name.

Charon.

He closes his eyes and kicks frantically away from the faces. It's not too late to reach the punt. It's not too far away.

Charon's chest aches fiercely. The water feels okay to breathe somehow, but that's another trap. If he lets it in, that's it.

Just a little farther...

His hand breaches the surface, grasping for another.

Nobody is around. Charon has to pull himself up out of the water.

His head emerges, and he takes in a massive breath. It burns his lungs. River water gets in his mouth. It's honey sweet, like mead.

"Father!"

The priest doesn't turn back. He pushes on, calling to the lost on shore.

Not the lost. Not anymore. The shepherd has returned to his flock.

And Charon? Charon is just another exorcised demon.

He treads water. He won't be able to keep it up much longer, but what the hell, he wants to see the priest get at least one of the penniless on the punt. Just one. Do what Charon never allowed.

The boy inside Charon cheers the priest on. The Charon that once was. The Charon that had to learn lessons the hard way, but learned them nonetheless.

Maybe this would be different.

Something brushes Charon's foot, but he kicks it away, his heel slipping into a mouth full of brittle teeth that break away like twigs.

"Come on."

The priest reaches shore and gestures to the left behind. The first one steps onto the punt, crying grateful tears.

Then the next one comes.

Then the next.

They swarm the priest, clamouring for room on the punt.

Charon can see the man yelling, but can't make out the words. Likely telling them he'll make the trip as many times it takes. He'll save them all.

But they don't listen. The punt dips. Water covers the back, slips over the gunwale.

It begins to sink.

They'll all be swimming, the priest included.

The priest looks out into the water. His wide, pleading eyes land on Charon.

Charon shrugs.

A screaming woman grabs at the priest and they both fall into the murk.

Soon, everyone is below the surface. Soon, Charon is the only one left. Tired legs and arms keeping himself afloat in the depths.

Something brushes against his foot. Something big.

He never expected to retire from this job, but occasionally he would dream about what such a time would look like. Maybe he'd be allowed into the afterlife. He had allowed himself to hope.

For a replacement. For someone to come and take the pole. Now someone has.

For all the wandering in purgatory the lost souls had done, none had languished there as long as Charon.

The water beneath him rises. Something is displacing it.

It's not just big: it's colossal. It's as if the ground is coming up to meet him. The living, breathing, hating ground.

Charon has forgotten how to fear. He misses his punt. The boy inside him curls into a ball.

Whimpering, Charon does the same.

⚰ ⚰ ⚰ ⚰ ⚰

CHRISTOPHER O'HALLORAN (he/him) is the factory-working, Canadian, actor-turned-author of PUSHING DAISY, his upcoming debut novel from Lethe Press (2025). His shorter work has been published or forthcoming from Kaleidotrope, NoSleep Podcast, Cosmic Horror Monthly, and others. He is editor of the anthology, Howls from the Wreckage. Visit COauthor.ca for stories, reviews, and updates on upcoming novels.

WHATEVER REMAINS OF ME

MICHAEL PICCO

The baby stopped crying sometime yesterday.

I can't say when exactly, because I honestly don't know. I get lost, you see. Lost in reverie. Time moves differently for me now. It's... stretched and ragged... distended and sluggish.

Like me, I suppose. Or, at least the *physical* me.

I didn't used to believe in ghosts. I didn't used to believe in zombies, either, but well, here we are. I seem to be both—a revenant's ghost, you might say. I'm all that remains of the humanity I once took for granted. You know, the rational, thinking part that's been removed from the thing that now shambles through the world. It's a strange sort of dichotomy: me and the thing that *used* to be me. The thing (or *things*, depending on your perspective) that *used* to be human.

Whatever you want to call us—ghost or spirit, shambler or zombie—the conscious part of me is powerless to do anything but bear witness to the monster I've become. And the zombie me is incapable of anything but feeding its appetite.

I don't know how long I've been tethered to this thing, this rotting shell that used to be my body. As I've said, time has lost all meaning for me. All I can say is I've been this way long enough to blunt any shock or horror about what my body continues to do. Well, that's not entirely true, if I'm being honest. *This can't be happening! This can't be real!* I say these things to myself often, over and over again. I repeat these phrases like a mantra; but they've become so worn down by repetition they have lost their meaning.

I've become so numb...so numb. My spirit has grown as cold and dead as my body; consumed not by rot, but by despair. Sometimes, it feels as though I'm watching events unfold from a thousand miles away...my own monstrosity is too much to bear.

I *should* be in shock—crazed—after all the things I've witnessed...by all the things I've done. My conscious self, my *ghost* self, recoils at my physical capacity for brutality. The sheer primal nature of it. It's during those times that my awareness retreats into a sort of vague and wary fugue, where hunger and violence and pain can no longer reach me. That's my only escape, my only refuge from the thing I've become.

Yes, it's too much...too much. The human mind can only stand so much savagery...so much *revulsion*. Perhaps, in my madness, my mind has conjured this elaborate ghostly fantasy to bulwark the last tattered remnants of my sanity.

Perhaps.

It *is* much more comforting to believe I've lost my mind than to ponder my own death, or worse still, my *undeath*. It is far easier to consider that I'm utterly deranged, than to accept that this is hell. Because I *am* in hell, even if I don't deserve to be. In my more lucid moments, I can't help but wonder if I'm even responsible for what the physical me does under the influence of the disease. Philosophers tell us that without consciousness, we cannot be held accountable for our actions. Without consciousness, without intent or malice, sin and morality become abstractions.

They become utterly irrelevant. Like ghosts. Like me.

It's a desperate rationale. Teetering here on the crumbling precipice of insanity, it's the only thing I have left to cling to.

The baby's arm tears free from his shoulder with a soft, wet crunch; his flawless skin stretching until, at last, the flesh and muscle are ripped into long bloody tatters. For an instant, I don't see it as a baby anymore. He's not even *human* anymore. He's just meat.

Yes...just sweet, sweet baby meat.

This thing's hunger...*my* hunger is insatiable. And, ghost or otherwise, I'm *starving.* The things I've become are both endlessly voracious. The hunger permeates my spectral awareness, making me an insatiable ghost, as improbable as that may seem.

As the gristle in his shoulder pops and crunches, I watch the other me's mouth water as it clumsily lifts the baby's ragged stump to its maw. Some sort of grisly black drool spills from the bullet hole in my jaw. This spatters onto the floor before it even takes its first bite. Not that my mouth has saliva or taste buds or even a functioning tongue anymore. I doubt its body—my body—is producing anything but more virus these days. Still, it is strange that I *feel* the burst of saliva swell beneath *my* tongue even before zombie me takes its first bite.

Like either of us even has functioning salivary glands.

I suspect the sensation is more sensory memory than actual perception. But really, there is no telling what my body experiences and what's being shared ("transmitted?") with my "ghost." Hunger, certainly—that's a constant; but also, the sensation of being exhausted. Utterly completely exhausted—a fatigue a thousand years' sleep couldn't satisfy. So, obviously, I still *feel* things: there's the odd and intermittent sights and sounds my body produces as it steadily rots away; there's the dull and pervasive pain of my shattered cheekbone; the nimble, but indelicate gnawing of the flies. These are the sorts of things I perceive both as a ghost and through the body it used to inhabit.

The dichotomy is more than a little disorienting.

I used to think it was the virus that would ultimately end up killing me—not the bullet through my head (which somehow missed my brain and took off most of my right cheekbone instead). But then, it wasn't *really* a "virus," was it? Not the terrestrial kind at least. While it shared *some* of the properties of a virus, scientists said it contained entire segments of DNA that were utterly alien. Before everything went to shit, they seemed to conclude it was some sort of bio-weapon. Something genetically engineered, but way beyond what humans were capable of creating. Some people simply called it "The Wrath of God," and that certainly fits. We are, all of us, cursed—living, dead and *undead*—trapped here, trapped in the dreadful liminality between life and death.

Before I died, I had hoped death might bring oblivion...some release from what I'd seen...from what I've done. But, it hasn't.

I have the baby clutched under my arm like a football. I drift in and out of awareness as the thing I've become gnaws and chews mindlessly on the flesh of his forearm. My response is probably a classic indicator of shock, but really, who understands the psychology of ghosts? I try to ignore the cartoon train on the sleeve of the baby's romper. It's not that difficult to do. Smilin' Toni The Train is almost completely lost in the blood stains. Despite the days of dehydration, the baby's flesh is still...you know: *juicy*. I know that's a terrible thing to say. It's a terrible thing to even *think*, right? Not that it matters either way. I can't tell anybody and it's not as though someone can tell what I'm thinking anyway. Besides, it's a wonder I can even think at all, after everything that's happened.

When I shot myself, I thought all my troubles would be over. *Sweet oblivion, here I come!* I remember thinking as I pulled the trigger. You see, I thought by locking myself in the bathroom, and putting a gun under my clammy chinny-chin-chin, I would prevent anybody else from getting hurt—or getting infected. By that time, I had already reached the point where I was too feverish, too delirious, to do anything about the baby. It wasn't like I could hand him off to his mother! I couldn't call a sitter! I couldn't just drop the baby off at my folks' place and shuffle off this mortal coil! That wasn't the way the world worked anymore. Everything had gone to shit so fast. It's a wonder the baby and I survived as long as we did.

I should have killed the baby before I turned the gun on myself. That would have been the kindest cut. Not that *that* would prevent what is happening now, I suppose, but it might make witnessing this a little easier.

I don't know what I was thinking; and, perhaps in my delirium, I simply *wasn't* thinking at all. I only vaguely remember bits of my life now: I was married to my college sweetheart; I had just become a father; I had a mortgage. You know: 'adulting' as the kids say. Anyway, a week after the outbreak, after my wife died, and returned from the dead hungry and inhuman, with the electricity gone and communications down, with *my* fever spiking...offing myself *seemed* the best solution at the time.

It was the end of the world, after all.

I vaguely remember spray painting: "HELP! Live baby inside!" on the side of the garage (or at least I think I did. There were so many things I did in those final hours that escape me now), but obviously, nobody got the message. No one came to our rescue. Now that I think about it, I don't know if I managed to actually *lock* myself in the bathroom. If I did, apparently, it wouldn't have mattered. After the virus took me, the baby's cries drove me into such a frenzy that I clawed and chewed through the door.

Maybe hollow-core doors weren't the best choice when my wife and I remodeled this place. That's how she got out of our bedroom...after she "changed" I mean. Like me, she was trying to get to the baby. After she got sick, the baby *never* stopped crying. Maybe there was some dim and remote flicker of maternal instinct still at work in her then, but I doubt it. She had become utterly crazed. Ravenous. Even after I shot her—once, twice, *three* times—she still managed to bite me.

I finally managed to pin her down, only a few feet from the crib. I put the barrel of the gun just under her right ear. It was a place I had kissed a thousand times before. It was quick. The gunshot seemed so loud. There was so much blood.

It was something I should have done hours before, but I just couldn't do it. I just *couldn't*. I really shouldn't beat myself up over something like that.

Or for the cheap doors, for that matter.

Before the outbreak, life with a new baby relegated our focus down to necessities and easy-to-make choices. Sleep deprivation played a huge part in our mental deterioration over the course of the last few months. My wife and I would joke we had become zombies, aimlessly wandering through a world of people who had somehow managed to master sleep and this whole parenting thing. How we longed to pick their brains—oh, their sweet, juicy brains!—to discover the secret to getting more than a few dodgy hours of sleep every night! We never thought that in just a few short months, we both would be *literal* zombies, navigating a very real apocalypse.

But then, how *do* you prepare for the end of the world? You don't. You can't. And it wouldn't be rational even if you could, right? The very notion of the undead defies everything we know about biology and physiology. Zombies are supernatural, the stuff of B-grade horror movies: thinly-veiled commentaries about consumerism, easily rendered morality tales about gluttony. The notion of zombies (or ghosts for that matter), was ridiculous. *Is* ridiculous…but, whatever.

I remember seeing the first report of the outbreak on the BBC, and turning to my wife and saying: "They're saying there are actual zombies in Barbados…."

"There's no such thing as zombies," she responded tiredly, mechanically stroking the baby's back as he slumped over her shoulder. I could tell she was irritated. The baby had become so fussy recently. He just wasn't sleeping…

"Right. But, there's footage—"

"It's got to be a hoax. The BBC is being punked."

But, as it turned out, the reporting was accurate. Unbelievable? Yes. Inexplicable? Also, yes. And the outbreak wasn't localized either. It all happened so fast, and it was *everywhere*. Reports started to come in from all over the world. By the time the BBC started covering the outbreak in Barbados, some of the more remote parts of the world had already succumbed. One French YouTuber posted a video of a police cordon being overrun. "*C'est fini—c'est fait! La Fin a commencé!*" he shouted over the footage, in an odd sing-song way. Despite being riddled with bullets, the infected overwhelmed the cordon in seconds. Europe went dark shortly thereafter.

That's another reason why I suspect the disease was an engineered virus. Nothing in nature spreads that quickly. Only an artificial virus would have that kind of communicability and that high of a fatality rate. Besides, nature is not going to produce something that kills its host only to bring it back to life again. That's absolutely redundant.

Or bloody brilliant.

The baby's tender knuckles grind and crunch underneath my ragged teeth. I can feel his finger bones dislodge and snap against my ragged tongue. The pain isn't inconsiderable, but hunger supersedes it. In the state I'm in, hunger eclipses *everything*. Thankfully, I'm spared most of the taste. There is the vaguest hint of salty, metallic blood, but, in the rust-rotted spectrum of sensation, that is a very minor perception. I suppose it's barely worthy of mention, but it illustrates what gets through to the conscious part of me these days.

I try to focus on something else—*anything* else. I need something to distract me, but my spectral gaze keeps getting drawn to my black and bloated hands.

I notice then that my fingers (which is to say, my *physical* body's fingers) have started to rot off. That would explain the dull ache that extends up my arms all the way to my elbows. The ache is occasionally offset by an excruciating jolt of pain as a digit rots off and tumbles to the ground. I lost an entire finger yesterday — my ring finger. My wedding band was nearly subsumed beneath the last knuckle. Oddly, the missing digit appears more ephemeral than the others on my ghost hand. It's become faded, even more ghostly than the rest of me.

I feel it—remotely and distantly, like you might if you stubbed a numbed toe—but, apparently, I'm the only one who does.

My body doesn't give any indication it feels pain or injury or, well, anything. All that matters to it is feeding the hunger. I say *feeding* it, because the hunger itself is never satisfied. Before the world went dark, scientists were saying the virus targeted the hypothalamus. That's the part of your brain that regulates appetite. And aggression.

The hypothalamus is the perfect target for an engineered super-virus.

I often wonder how this will all end. I suppose someone might find me here, and shoot me. As long as they're better with a gun than I was, I say have at it! Otherwise, I suspect my bodily deterioration will not only continue, but accelerate, the rot consuming my limbs before my body finally falls apart completely. Maybe then, and only then, I will find true death...some small peace in oblivion. But then, that theory wasn't borne out by my suicide attempt, so my expectations are pretty low.

I won't starve, that's for sure. It feels like I will, even though I'm gorging myself on baby meat. But then, I'm not actually *digesting* what I'm eating, am I? I'm not metabolizing it, I mean. The flesh I consume is simply accumulating in my bowels — getting more and more compacted with every grisly bite I take. Everything I eat is putrefying along with the rest of my organs. What happens when the rotting tissue in my stomach can no longer bear the burden of my appetite? Will my abdomen burst? Already, my torso has become so distended I can no longer "see" my own feet. At least, not from the zombie's vantage.

I wonder sometimes if the virus causes hallucinations, too. In the mad world I now inhabit, I see strange things: wisps of figures that flit into and out of the shadows. At first, I thought perhaps these were other ghosts, people who, like me, had succumbed to the virus only to be "reincarnated" as phantoms. But the ghostly things I perceive aren't human. Their proportions are wrong. They have too many limbs; too many mouths. The way they move is unnatural. They skitter and glide through the empty streets like some enormous species of water strider. Perhaps, they are the ones who caused all this, but what they might be (Aliens? Demons? Ghosts? Interdimensional beings?), I really couldn't say. I wonder sometimes if my zombie self senses them, too. I've seen its head twitch whenever one of these things make an appearance. But then, given the deterioration of its eyes, it's a wonder it can see anything.

Soft, moist tissue was one of the first things the maggots targeted after I shot myself. While the fall chill has killed most of them off, I can still feel them burrowing into my sinuses. Occasionally, I will sense one squirming as it drops down the back of my throat. It flails and squirms on the back of my tongue for a moment and then it's gone. But the larvae don't die; at least, not all of them do. They tend to emerge, fully pupated, whenever my body belches up some of the intestinal gas that has been percolating and collecting in my guts. They are propelled out of my mouth on a wave of putrescence and bits of black carrion which splatter over the freshly painted walls of the nursery. The poor creatures that make it through the expulsion fling themselves against the windows, braining themselves against the glass over and over until they die.

I think these flies are little pieces of my soul. They want to escape from this world, too.

A dreadful sigh escapes the baby's blackened lips. Indelicately, I grasp the baby by its chubby leg and hold it up at arm's length. Partially coagulated blood drips from its mangled shoulder. The baby twitches and begins to snap and bite at me, even before its eyes open. Zombie me drops it to the floor where it lands with a sickening thud. The baby wails and actually hisses at me, gnawing toothlessly on my ankle. My wife would be appalled by me dropping our child, but I suspect that isn't the worst thing that's going to happen to him.

Or to whatever remains of me.

Michael Picco is an award-winning author based in Colorado. He has been hooked on horror since third grade, when he was first exposed to the works of H.P. Lovecraft. His writing has since been influenced by authors such as Stephen King, Ray Bradbury, Stephen R. Donaldson and Dan Simmons. Over the last ten years, Michael has contributed to nearly twenty anthologies and has also produced two short-story collections and a full-length novel. His work has been appeared in the U.S. and abroad and has received accolades for its nuanced and unsettling style of story telling.

BAPTISM

KELLY PINER

As the giant red disc in the sky burned away the early morning haze, Burt Murdock finished his third cup of coffee at Starlight Diner, situated in the Lowcountry of South Carolina. A 1959 calendar on the wall sported a picture of a pin-up girl in a red bikini, holding a Pepsi. He wouldn't have stopped, except his eyes were as heavy as two bricks. He'd driven straight through the night after his sister, Kay, had phoned.

"He doesn't have long," she'd said.

Now, as Burt fought exhaustion, he glanced at his watch and figured that if he only stopped for gas, he could make it home to say his goodbyes and pay his respects.

Their father had lived with Kay until his lung cancer had returned, six months ago. Now, a mere shadow of his former self, he lingered at Saint Mary's Nursing Home. Burt choked back his regrets: too few visits, always something more important to do. Now, with only hours left, he'd try to say all the words that had gone unsaid over the years. How he regretted the petty jealousies and disagreements, and all for what?

He handed the cashier two ones and said, "Keep the change. Where's your pay phone?"

"Sorry, hon, but it's been out of order for nearly a week. If you go about ten miles down the road, there's a gas station on the right. You'll find one there."

He returned to his car, more eager than ever to speak with Kay. Their father could have died during the night. Panic gripped his chest. Soon, he may be making funeral arrangements.

To shut out his thoughts, he cranked up the radio of his new '59 Chevy. But as hard as he tried, he couldn't quiet his mind. He had three big sales jobs lined up for the week, and now he may have to miss work. Timmy's college tuition was due in a month, but without the commissions...

But what kind of man worried about business meetings when his dad lay on his death bed? He'd never forgotten the disappointment on his father's face the day he'd told him he wouldn't be joining the family business. His dad had assumed Burt would be his partner aboard his fishing trawler, *The Ebb Tide*, but Burt had accompanied his father enough to know life at sea wasn't for him. He had envisioned a different future, an office with a secretary and nice suits and ties. Burt would have never made it as a fisherman, but still, it had created a rift with his father that had never healed. He took a deep breath and focused on the winding two-lane highway.

That's when he spotted the small church, situated back from the road, surrounded by moss-covered trees. Never a religious man, he couldn't understand his sudden urge to stop. But he felt an inexplicable sense of urgency, as if God were directing him there.

He turned into a gravel parking lot and read a fading sign, *Salvation Holiness Church.* About 25 parishioners had gathered on the front lawn dressed in their Sunday finest, women in stunning hats adorned with colorful flowers and ribbons, and men in tailored suits and crisp dress shirts. Burt hoped the congregation didn't mind him intruding upon their service.

He tucked his keys into his pocket and walked toward an official-looking man wearing a black robe. He extended his right hand. "I'm Burt Murdock. I hope you don't mind, I'm traveling to visit my dying father and felt a strong need for prayer."

The intensity of the minister's gaze unsettled Burt, caused him to second-guess his decision to stop, but then the minister's face lit up as he took Burt's hand.

"Reverend Peterson. Welcome, Brother. We've been expecting you."

Burt locked eyes with the minister. A strange remark, he thought, from a man he'd never met, but perhaps the reverend was only trying to put him at ease. "Thank you," he replied.

The preacher placed his hand on Burt's back. "Come with me."

Inside the tiny church, ten wooden benches rested on each side of a narrow strip of worn red carpet that ran down the aisle to the altar. A large oil painting of Jesus being crucified hung behind the pulpit.

Reverend Peterson motioned. "Please, sit in the front pew. You'll get a special ordinance today."

How long since Burt had attended church, maybe twenty years? As the congregation settled around him, several members waved to Burt and shouted, "Welcome," over the roar of an oscillating fan.

Burt's unease returned. He felt naked, sitting up front for all to see. And just what had the reverend meant about the special ordinance?

Reverend Peterson raised his arms, palms up, as an elderly woman played "Amazing Grace" on an old pump organ. Unable to locate a hymn book, Burt mouthed the few words he could remember from so many years ago.

"You may be seated," the minister said, after the last verse had been sung. He ran his gaze over Burt. "We have a very special guest today, Mr. Burt Murdock, led here by none other than God almighty himself."

Burt bristled when a flurry of "Hallelujahs," echoed from behind him. He hadn't wanted to be the center of attention. He'd only wanted a few prayers for his dad.

"Brother Burt, please come to the altar and tell us how we can help."

Burt felt glued to his seat, like he was being called on to read aloud from a book report he hadn't written. He resisted an urge to flee the church. But what if Reverend Peterson was right, that he'd been beckoned by God to stop and pray?

So he stood on stiff legs and ambled to the front. From there, he looked into the serious faces of thirty or more parishioners. "Thank you for welcoming me into your church. The truth is, I'm not a religious man. But today, on my way to see my dying father, I felt a strong need for prayer."

A woman in the back waved her arms in the air and shouted, "Praise, God."

Burt wasn't accustomed to such an expressive congregation, a far cry from the restrained Episcopal churched he'd attended as a child.

"Tell us your father's name?" the minister asked.

"Ralph Murdock."

Reverend Peterson raised his head to the ceiling. "Our heavenly Father, please look over Brother Ralph and bestow your gifts upon him. You have directed his son to us today so that life may be restored to his father."

Burt blanched. His father was dying. He doubted anyone could "restore life" to him.

"What we need is an old-fashioned baptism," Reverend Peterson bellowed.

"Amen to that," the congregation responded.

Burt struggled to find a graceful exit. He'd thank them for their prayers, but this wasn't what he'd wanted. He was wasting time when he needed to be on his way.

But before he could react, the congregation moved toward him. The church organist handed him a robe and pointed to a back room. "You can change in there."

His mind went foggy as he got swept up in the group, eager to lead him through some unknown ritual. All he knew of a baptism was a priest sprinkling a few drops of water onto someone's head. But it felt wrong to offend them; they'd been so gracious. Reluctantly, he went into the small room and slipped out of his clothes and into the full-length robe. He'd seen TV programs where churches had shallow pools inside for baptisms. That would explain the robe. This wouldn't take long, and then he'd drive away.

When he emerged, wearing his robe, the congregation led him outside, toward the woods. As the overhead sun vanished inside the curtained forest, an eager murmur shot through the crowd. What fate awaited him? Burt wanted to ask questions, but he felt woozy and disoriented. Their voices, like undulating waves, became slushy and muddled. It had to be the shock of the whole situation, the oddness of events.

It'll be over soon, Burt reminded himself.

The group walked farther and farther into the forest, down a path filled with honeysuckle and barberry bushes. The chatter of marsh wrens reverberated against the forest wall.

Then Burt saw it, a great expanse with a sparkling creek, spiritual and surreal, that appeared out of nowhere: the kind of place where John the Baptist might have baptized Jesus. Frogs leapt from log to log and turtles paddled past.

Reverend Peterson led the group to an embankment. "Brother Burt, step forward."

Without thinking, Burt removed his shoes, and Reverend Peterson led him into the middle of the creek.

The coolness of the water felt good against Burt's flesh. A rainbow, like a multicolored kaleidoscope, filled the morning sky. Burt wondered if this was what being *Born Again* meant.

The minister held a cross over Burt's head. "Lord Jesus, forgive this man for his sins."

"Forgive this man for his sins," the congregation repeated.

And then, members of the congregation removed their shoes and entered the creek, women in their dresses and the men in suits.

Burt didn't understand it. Was this what Reverend Peterson had meant by an old-fashioned baptism? He watched parishioners move toward him.

The congregation chanted, "Repent your sins, Brother. Repent your sins, so that your father may have life."

Burt's feet sank deeper and deeper into the muddy bottom so that now the water met his chin. He hadn't come here to repent his sins.

Burt shut his eyes and prayed for salvation. He hadn't known it would be this way. He'd only wanted a few prayers. Trapped, he hoped to wake up and find himself back in his own bed. He turned to Reverend Peterson for some hint of what was happening, but the minister's eyes had turned black and glassy.

"Confess your sins, Brother, so that your father may have everlasting life."

Burt sobbed and a voice from deep inside himself confessed every sin he'd ever committed, from stealing a candy bar when he'd been five to his tawdry affair with his secretary. And when he had finished, the congregation shouted, "Praise, Jesus."

Reverend Peterson placed his hand on Burt's head and plunged him backward into the creek as he recited, "In the name of the Father, the Son, and the Holy Ghost."

Burt struggled to free himself, but the reverend's hold was too strong. Never a good swimmer, he held his breath, but he felt his life slipping away. In the water, dead marine life floated past, followed by Burt's dead relatives, including the decaying bodies of his grandmother and mom. As he watched his relatives pass, he wondered if he had been banished to hell.

Sweat dribbled from Burt's forehead and soaked the front of his shirt as he squinted into the searing afternoon sun and looked around. He recognized the parking lot of the small church. But the lot was empty without a single soul in sight.

The weird baptism, Reverend Peterson, the congregation, where were they?

Burt pressed a handkerchief to his face. Just goes to show, he thought, what sleep deprivation can do. He'd obviously pulled over into the parking lot for a nap. It was the only explanation. And what a nightmare! He looked at his watch, one pm. If he hit the road, he'd pull into his hometown by five. There might still be time to rush to his father's side and ask for forgiveness: for his selfishness, for all the things he'd never said.

He gunned the engine, each small town blending into the next, while he worried that his dad had died while he'd napped away the morning. When he finally saw the *Welcome to Marshville* sign, his concern increased. He was so close now, only minutes away from the nursing home. Would he make it?

It looked different somehow, Saint Mary's Care Center. He'd only been there twice, but he could have sworn the building had been a radiant yellow, not dingy grey. He raced down the corridor, searching for his dad's name posted outside any door.

He was searching for help when a nurse emerged from the bathroom across the hall carrying a bed pan, her face ashen.

"Nurse, can you tell me locate my father, Ralph Murdock?"

But she walked right past, seeming not to hear him.

"Nurse? Nurse?" She was obviously preoccupied, he thought.

Burt then noticed a funeral announcement attached to a cork board.

Please join us at Saint Peter's Church at 1:00 p.m. on Sunday May 21, 1959 to honor Brother Ralph Murdock.

Burt pressed his hand to his mouth. My God! But his dad was alive last night. Today was only Sunday. How could his dad have died and have a service on the same day? And just where was Kay?

The clock at the end of the hallway read: 12:30 p.m..

If he rushed, he could make it to the funeral in time.

Unable to quiet his pounding heart, Burt sped to the church, ignoring stop signs and the only traffic light in town. He couldn't have napped through his father's death and funeral preparations. It wasn't possible.

From the paved lot of the church, Burt gaped at six pall-bearers rolling a gurney through the front lawn and toward the woods in the back, a white sheet draped over a body. Reverend Peterson followed behind, holding a cross high in the air. In the distance, the congregation from Salvation Holiness stood in attendance.

Burt rested his face in his hands. He had to be losing his mind. He just had to be.

Kay and her husband followed the procession.

"Kay! Kay!" Burt yelled.

As if in slow motion, he struggled to join her as the gurney was pushed down a narrow trail, past tangled weeds and poison ivy. A murky creek emerged beyond the bald cypress trees.

Reverend Peterson grabbed the corpse under its arms and moved into the middle of the stream.

Burt had never attended such a funeral and whimpered when he recognized his father's decaying body, appearing weeks old, not just one day.

He tried to reach Kay, but his legs felt trapped in quick sand.

Reverend Peterson looked up at the sky. "Our Heavenly Father, we are here today so that life can be restored to Brother Ralph."

"Amen," the congregation responded.

"For God so loved the world that he gave his only begotten son, Brother Burt Murdock, so that Ralph could have everlasting life." Reverend Peterson dunked the body's head three times into the creek while reciting, "In the name of the Father, the Son and the Holy Ghost."

"No!" Burt screamed. He hadn't meant to sacrifice his own life. He'd only wanted to ease his dad's suffering; maybe help him cross over into the light. But not this. Reverend Peterson had misunderstood. Was it too late to take it all back and makes things right? He swallowed his terror.

And then, Burt's father coughed and moaned, and his head and arms moved as if he'd been newly born. He'd been brought to life, resurrected.

"Hallelujah!" the congregation cried.

When Burt looked down, his body had disappeared beneath him.

Kelly Piner is a Clinical Psychologist who in her free time, tends to feral cats and searches for Bigfoot in nearby forests. Her writing is inspired by Rod Serling's *Twilight Zone*. *Most recently*, Ms. Piner's story, "Euthanasia," was chosen as *The Best of 2023* by *After Dinner Conversation*. Her short stories have appeared in *Litro Magazine, Scarlet Leaf Review, Dragon Soul Press, The Last Girl's Club/Wicked News, Rebellion Lit Review, The Chamber Magazine, Drunken Pen Writing, Lit Shark Magazine, The Literary Hatchet, Weirdbook, Written Tales and others.* Her stories have also appeared in multiple anthologies.

Annie May

Corrine Pridmore

Musky. Wet. Concrete gritted against my cheek. The cold stone pressed against my jaw.

"Oh...God..." The sentence was somewhere between a cough and gasp.

Everything *ached*. Muscles throbbed in my temple. Cramping tremors tightened along my diaphragm and stomach. Breaths came in catches that whistled through lungs that hadn't quite decided whether they worked. I was pretty sure ribs were broken from the fall.

The fall. Hazy memories formed along the edge of my consciousness. Two bodies, a haphazard grin. What was I doing here? *Where* the hell was I? Where was Adin?

Adin, I need you. Help me...

I tried to push myself up with my arms and bit back a whimper, listening to my wrist crack against the weight. Broken.

A small voice screamed in the back of my mind, *"Shhhh, oh God, be quiet! Don't let them hear you. Whatever you do, you can't let him find you."*

It took everything I had, a deep recess of strength I didn't even realize existed, to lift up again on my uninjured arm. The elbow shook, threatening to spill the weight. With a slowness born out of stubbornness, I got to my knees.

Where am I?

I was in a room where the only light came from the crack at the bottom of a door several feet above my head. The air tasted damp and old, and what little light was provided showed cracked concrete, windowless walls.

A basement?

"Are you alright? That was a nasty fall you took, Miss."

The voice was low, feminine and worried. All the same, the sound made my heart shudder. I tried to find who spoke through the small stream of light, but all I could see was the rusted tools that made crooked shapes—like tombstones against the horizon.

"Please," I whispered, unsure if the woman could hear the quiet plea. "Please, please, *please* be quiet—"

"He's gone for now, Miss." A soft scraping sound, chains clinking. "They both are, but it ain't long until they return. Not long at all."

"I—" I swallowed. *It's not just me, is it? God, Adin.* "No, *we*, we've got to get out of here."

A soft, despondent laugh. "'fraid there's not much luck for me either way."

Her voice was soft, whispery in the way that only southern accents were. How she found herself in the middle of New York, I wasn't sure I even wanted to know.

"I don't....*understand*..." More memories were coming back now in painful flashes that made me whimper. I remembered the couple stranded on the highway, how my fiancé, Adin, had decided to stop and try to help them because he'd seen the car seat in the back.

"*How could they?*"

The chains clinked more, and I could hear iron scrape against concrete. On the edge of the dirty light, there was movement. A small shape rose from the edge of the wall and stumbled toward me, bringing the sound of moving iron and metal and stone with it.

"Funny how things work, ain't it?" she said. I caught glimpses of short, dirty blond hair, and as she got closer, I saw how the tattered sundress struggled to stay on the starved body. Despite her depraved condition, there was something in her eyes—pale blue in the light—that screamed *life*. "Men much crueler than animals ever thought to be, yes. Must be 'cause men can think."

"They...killed..." I couldn't stop the sobs. They rose from a part that went deeper than my soul, from somewhere that reached past everything but the pain. I couldn't stop the pitiful sounds, no matter how afraid I was that they would find me, how afraid *he* would find me. The cries hurt my cracked ribs, lancing pain through my chest and throbbing head—and still I cried.

"There, there." She reached out her hands that were shackled by rusted metal and despite myself I leaned into the stranger, feeling her collarbone through her skin as she tucked my face into her chest.

"He's dead."

"Sooner or later we all leave those we love," she whispered. "Don't you dare think that don't mean he ain't watchin' you. You need to pull yourself together now. If not for you, you hafta for him."

Run, protect yourself and grieve later. Easy to think, but so much harder for me to do. There were only the horrific images of Adin's death replaying in my thoughts as I cried. So quickly, they'd taken him—and in such a painful manner.

It took a moment, but something about how her hand ran through my hair calmed me. A strange smell—like roses after a few days of being picked—seemed to linger around her. A sickly-sweet smell of decay and flowers.

"What do we do?" I whispered. "How can I get you out of those chains?"

She gave me a sad, knowing smile that I couldn't quite comprehend. "There's nothing you can do for me now." She took my wrist, and I bit back a whimper as she laid it against her lap. She ripped a piece off the bottom of her blue sundress with the dirty white lace. Grabbing an old handle to some forgotten tool, she placed it against my arm and wrapped it tightly with the cloth to create a makeshift splint.

"We've gotta get you out of here."

I shook my head. "No. I can't leave without you." I clung to her arm with my good hand. The stranger who I already loved more than I could understand shook her head.

"And what do you propose to do? Cut these here chains? If you can leave and get help, get the police, then that will help me more than watching them torture you." Her eyes—sad and lost—pierced me. "I've seen enough of that here in this hell."

I knew her words made sense. I knew in my condition, I couldn't free her. Despite that, I hated that I even considered leaving without her. I could feel myself nod against my will. "How do I get out?"

She pointed above my head at our sole source of light coming from the crack of the closed door. There were no stairs to it, and the light showed bloody scratch marks where someone had tried to escape before.

"I can help lift you up there but mind your arm." She stood and linked her arms through my shoulder to help me stand. After a moment of waiting, she let me go where I wavered before standing straighter. The pain in my chest had lessened, adrenaline and fear numbing everything except for the deep sorrow Adin had left.

"He's gone..." I whisper.

"Don't think about it now. You can mourn later." Her voice had grown in urgency. "I can't rest unless you help me stop them."

"I don't understand—"

"You ain't the first, and, honey, you won't be the last." She put a hand on the back of my head. "I was their first and they've kept me here since. Twelve other girls I've watched them kill. But you? You're special." Her tone had turned excited and almost manic. "I can *feel* it. You've got a will to live that's somethin' powerful." She pushed me toward the door high above us. The remnants of a banister could be seen against a wall, but the stairs seemed to have long been torn down. A tall door made of heavy oak, seven feet above my head, stood between me and possible freedom. "Now you've got roundabout twenty minutes to get outta this house. Watch for their car and go to the first house you see. Don't stop, and don't worry about me. The cops can help me better than you can. You understand?"

I nodded and fished my foot through her looped hands. She lifted me with relative ease, and I had a moment to wonder where the starved woman got her strength. My hurt hand hit against the brass doorknob and barely steadied myself as I opened it and pushed my torso through the doorway.

"Pride broke them, it did," I heard her say in breathless triumph. "Thought that just 'cause they didn't have stairs that their girls couldn't get out."

I lay on the linoleum floor, blinking into the blaring kitchen light for a moment. Everything was too sunny, too...*normal*...to equate to the ancient basement I'd just escaped from. I stood and leaned over the entranceway, looking for the stranger who had helped me out. Even though the kitchen light flooded the basement, there was nothing.

"Are you there?"

"Where else am I gonna go?" her voice flooded back, strong and alive, and I couldn't help but smile.

"I'm coming back with help, I promise," I said. "I can't tell you how much this means to me. When we get out of this you and I can sit down..."

"You need to go," she interrupted. Now her voice sounded pained and sad. "Please..."

I didn't answer her, turning to leave before she said, "Wait, Genevieve."

"—how did you know my—"

"I'm Annie May Johnson and I need you to tell my folks down in Kentucky that I'm sorry. I shoulda never ran off with that man. They were right, all those years ago. They were right. Will you do that for me? Tell them I was real brave and real strong and real kind just like they taught me to be."

"Annie May, don't talk like that—"

"Will you?" she interrupted again.

Time was getting short, and she sounded desperate so I said, "Yes, I will."

"Promise me, Genevieve."

"I promise."

"That's good." Her voice was softer. "Now you go on and live your life and tell my folks they'll see me soon enough."

There was a rattling sigh, a chink and clink as chains fell, and a rushing wind. "Annie May?"

No answer.

For a moment I stood there, repeating her name and praying for a response before I backed away and ran, leaving the door to the basement open.

6 months later

The small air conditioning unit allowed some reprieve from the summer heat, and I was glad for that. I sat in the living room filled with aging pictures of Annie May, waiting for her mother to return with the coffee. Annie May didn't look any older than when I'd seen her, even though the pictures were taken before 1985.

"The police told me what you said, Miss..."

"Please, you should just call me Genevieve," I replied, smiling and thanking her for the coffee. She sat on the chair beside me and looked at me through aged eyes that echoed Annie May's.

"They believe that you were hallucinating, that the fall you took made you see my daughter."

I nodded. "They wouldn't let me speak to you. They were afraid of how you would react." I cleared my voice. "I'm not even sure how I'm coping, and I barely knew her."

"I don't want to seem rude, but you couldn't have known my daughter. She disappeared near twenty-five years ago." For a moment the old woman was silent. "The police said that the couple killed her the week after they'd abducted her."

"I know what it seems like, and I know it sounds impossible, but your daughter helped me out of that basement."

She looked at me, tears pooling into the crevices and wrinkles around her eyes. "That's real cruel, Miss."

"My arm was broken, my ribs were cracked—" I took a deep breath and tried to keep the memories away, counting to three like my therapist said would help. Of course, it didn't really. "I had a severe concussion and the door was seven feet above me. How do you think I could have gotten out without help? Your daughter told me what to do and she hoisted me up and out of that basement. Annie May saved my life."

The old lady took a deep breath. "I think it's time you left, Miss."

I shook my head and set the coffee down on the coaster on the old wooden table. I reached out and the woman didn't try to stop me from taking her hand. "I *promised* her I would come find you." I spoke quickly to make sure she didn't interrupt. "She wanted me to tell you she was sorry for leaving with that man and that you and your husband were right and she was sorry." I smiled, feeling the tears crawling down my face. "She wanted you to know how brave, strong and kind she was, just like you taught her to be."

Before she could say anything else I fished the aging blue cloth out of my purse, feeling the coarse denim and old lace. I hesitated for a moment, fingers gripping the aged cloth. This was all I had left to comfort me—I'd tied it around my cast at Adin's funeral.

Let it go. I handed it to Annie May's mother.

The woman's hand shook as she clenched the dress fabric in her mottled hand. "Dear lord," she whispered.

"Annie May wrapped my wrist in it so I could get away," I said, my voice soft. The woman's shoulders began to shake with sobs that I was more than familiar with. I couldn't help but be reminded of how Annie May had comforted me when I leaned forward and hugged her crying mother.

"I'm sorry," I whispered. "I'm so sorry you had to lose her."

Movement in my peripheral vision caught my attention and I looked to see Annie May standing at the doorway, a small smile on her face.

"Thank you," she whispered. A moment later, a flash of white light, and she was gone.

Corrine Pridmore's passion for storytelling has been a lifelong endeavor. Their works explore the darker aspects of fiction, incorporating a range of genres that include horror, paranormal, sci-fi, and fantasy. Corrine delves into the depths of the human imagination to uncover what lurks within and strives for diversity and inclusion in their work. When not writing, they spend time caring for their menagerie of pets and reading about new realms on the horizon. Corrine finds a special sort of calm in their Appalachian Mountains. Other examples of their published work can be found on their website corrineprid-more.com.

Best Friends Forever

Stetson Ray

Ted's life was over.

His best friend Martin was dead, and it was his fault.

He was desperate for sleep, but every time he closed his eyes the memory of Martin's funeral replayed in his mind. The grim exhibition had dragged on for an eternity. Ted had sat in the back of the funeral home by himself, and the other mourners ignored him for the most part. He had felt like a dead dog lying on the roadside that nobody wanted to bury. Shunned. Overlooked. No one seemed to care about him anymore—not even his parents, who didn't even attend the funeral. Did they blame him for Martin's death? Probably. Everyone else did.

"I'm sorry," he said to his empty bedroom. "What else am I supposed to say? I'm sorry." He lay motionless in his bed, hating how powerless he felt. It wasn't fair. He was just a twelve year old kid. Just because Martin was dead didn't mean his mother and father were allowed to love him any less. "It wasn't my fault!" he screamed, then found himself repeating the four words until his throat burned.

When his bedroom door flung open and his father flipped on the light, Ted stopped yelling. His father watched from the doorway for a moment, then slowly lowered his head and stared at the floor. He looked as lost as Ted felt; he didn't seem to be angry, only sad and empty. After a moment, he spoke:

"I'm sorry all this happened to you, Teddy. If there was anything I could do to change it, I would."

He turned off the lights and closed the door, leaving Ted alone again. Ted rolled over and faced the wall and began to cry. Part of him wished he was the one who died. He wasn't looking forward to living the rest of his life riddled with guilt and shame and regret.

Around midnight, he drifted toward sleep. On the doorstep of a dream, he heard a noise—loud enough to pierce the fog of his slumber, but not loud enough to wake him entirely.

Again, but louder.

A clinking against glass.

High, bright, and impossible to ignore.

After it became clear the irritating noise wasn't going to stop, Ted sat up and opened his eyes.

Peering inside Ted's window, was Martin. More surprising than seeing his friend again was the feeling that came with it: instead of being afraid, Ted found he was glad to see his buddy.

Martin motioned for Ted to come to the window, but Ted couldn't move.

"Come on, open up," Martin said, his voice muffled by the glass.

Again he motioned with his hand. Ted slid out of bed and crossed the room and pushed the window up and squatted down. Eye to eye, the boys faced each other. It really was Martin. He looked completely normal except for his skin, which under the moonlight seemed a shade too pale.

"What are you doing here?" Ted asked. "You're supposed to be dead."

"What's that supposed to mean?" Martin grinned.

"You died. I went to your funeral. You were definitely dead."

"What are you talking about? You're seriously acting weird right now."

"You promise you're not dead?"

"I don't know what's up with you, but here, see for yourself." Martin punched Ted on the arm. "If I was dead, could I do that?"

"I'm not sure." Ted reached out and poked Martin on the chest with one finger. It felt like a normal chest. "I guess not."

"Knock it off, weirdo." Martin smacked Ted's hand away.

"So...are you a ghost?" Ted asked, and anger flashed across Martin's face.

"This isn't funny, Theodore. If all this dead stuff is some kind of joke, I don't get it, and I don't like it."

Ted didn't know what else to say. If Martin didn't know he was dead, then he didn't know how to convince him of it, so he decided to stop pressing the subject.

"Sorry," Ted said. "I was just kidding around."

"Your idea of a joke is lame." Martin seemed to relax.

They watched each other and listened to the crickets and cicadas for a moment.

"So...what's up?" Ted asked.

"I couldn't sleep, so I thought maybe we could go to the rocks again. It's so bright tonight we won't even need flashlights." Martin nodded up toward the full moon, and Ted's heart plummeted. "I think we should try to climb that big rock again."

"You remember...climbing the big rock?" Ted asked, a lump forming in his throat.

"Of course I do. It was just a day or two ago. I know we didn't make it to the top, but I have a good feeling about tonight. I think we can do it this time."

Apparently Martin could recall climbing the rock, but didn't remember falling off it—or more importantly, breaking his neck when he had landed.

"You wanna go or not?" Martin asked.

"Yeah," Ted replied, surprising himself.

"Then let's go before we wake up your parents."

Martin backed away from the window.

Feeling like a passenger inside his own body, Ted crawled out of his warm, safe bedroom to go on an adventure in the dark.

They snuck through the neighborhood as though nothing had happened. Martin seemed to be having a great time. Ted watched him with a suspicious eye, but Martin didn't appear to be dead. He wasn't see-through; he didn't stink; his neck was straight and unshattered. By the time they reached the edge of the neighborhood and entered the forest, Ted was having fun and feeling like himself again, but upon reaching their destination, his mood changed.

The rocks sat perched like tombstones on top of the ridge, pale gray under the silver moon light. Seeing the stone pillars horrified Ted, but what frightened him more was the overwhelming compulsion he felt to climb them.

"Am I dreaming?" Ted asked.

"I don't think so," the coffin jockey replied.

The rocky ridge in front of them was only about fifty feet tall and easy enough to climb, but four big boulders sat on top of the wall—the real challenge. Over the years, Ted and Martin had made it to the top of every rock except the biggest one. It was twice as tall as the others, its pinnacle rising at least seventy feet above the crest of the ridge. The monolith bulged in the middle and was flat on top, kind of like a giant mushroom. Ted and Martin had made it to the round bulge a few times, but could never make it any higher. On their previous attempt, Ted had finally reached the top, but Martin had not.

"We're going to make it this time, Teddy. I promise. I can feel it." Martin went to the base of the rocky ridge and stood there, waiting for Ted to join him.

Ted had given up trying to make sense of what was happening, but he was sure of one thing: he had to go first, just like last time. After taking a deep breath, he stumbled up to the wall, found a handhold, and began to climb.

Ted wondered what would happen when they reached the place where Martin fell. Would Martin remember? Would things go differently? Before he could think about it too much, he reached the base of the bulge.

The rock angled out slightly, making it impossible to use his feet for support until he could get past the round hump. To get up and over would require six or seven feet of climbing using nothing but the strength of his arms, and looking at the curve, Ted wondered how he got past it before.

With a shaky hand, he reached up and found a grip and pulled himself up. Just before his feet left the rock, his grip broke and he nearly lost his balance. Heart racing, he pressed his face against the wall and hugged the rock. The wind picked up and suddenly everything felt too real. Playtime was over. Coming with Martin had been a mistake. Drowning in fear, Ted called down to Martin, his voice trembling:

"I can't do it, Martin! I have to go down! I can't do this!"

From somewhere below, Martin calmly said, "Come on, Teddy, you've done it before. Remember? You can do this!"

Ted looked down and could see Martin looking up expectantly, his eyes pleading for Ted to continue, but Ted had lost faith in himself.

"That's the problem!" he cried, the wind roaring in his ears. "I can't remember how I did it! All I can remember is you falling, and the sound it made when you hit the ground!"

Watching from below, Martin looked a bit dispirited, but unafraid.

"Don't worry about me," Martin said. "Just find a good hand hold and don't look back until you get to the top."

"But what about you? What if you fall?"

"I won't. As long as you keep going, I'll be okay—I promise."

Ted wasn't sure why, but he trusted Martin. He looked up and found a place to stick his hand. He pulled and his feet swung away from the rock. He reached and jammed his fingers into another crack and pulled. He found a fist-sized divot and pulled again. He heaved his body over the hump and dug his feet into the rock and it was done.

Ted could barely believe the hardest part was over, but the climb wasn't finished, and he couldn't stop thinking about Martin. He decided to stay where he was rather than continuing on like before. He would wait on his friend, and maybe that would make a difference. Maybe the climb was some kind of second chance, and maybe he could save Martin this time.

But as he waited, over and over he heard the horrible crunching sound in his head.

Looking down, he could see nothing beyond the round part of the rock.

Then, moving with surprising speed, Martin effortlessly scrambled over the hump.

"Told you I wouldn't fall," Martin said with an attitude, waiting beside Ted.

"What happens now?" Ted asked.

"What do you think? We gotta keep going. We can't just stay here."

"Right."

Ted climbed toward the summit. He was almost sure he was dreaming. Or that Martin was a ghost. Or maybe a zombie. Regardless, getting to the top of the rock seemed to be the only thing that mattered. As he climbed, he tried to remember what happened after he reached the summit on the day that Martin fell, but could not; he couldn't even recall how he'd gotten down from the rock. After another minute or so of climbing, he found himself struggling to make it over the lip of the rock onto the flat summit.

A swift terror consumed him. His body and mind betrayed him. He couldn't think or breathe. He lost the ability to use his arms or legs. As he clung to the edge hoping he wouldn't fall, a shattered memory began to reassemble itself in his mind.

Ted knew exactly what would happen when his grip failed: the sudden feeling of weightlessness, the harrowing and inescapable sensation that comes with falling. He heard the wind screaming past him and saw the ground racing up to meet him.

Only a second away from losing his grip, a hand closed around Ted's wrist and hauled him over the lip and to his feet.

There was something different about Martin. He seemed sad and happy at the same time. They stood there on the summit of the rock, watching each other.

"Do you remember what happened?" Martin asked over the howling wind.

Ted desperately tried to push the memory away but couldn't; climbing the rock had cleared the fog from his mind. He shook his head no, but had the feeling Martin could tell he was lying.

"I'm sorry, Ted, but neither one of us made it," Martin said. "We both fell."

Hearing what he already knew was a punch in the gut.

"That can't be right. You fell. You're the one who died. I'm sorry Martin, but I lived. I made it to the top."

Ted tried to believe his own words, but it was becoming harder and harder to cling to the lie. He went to the edge of the rock, looked down, and his mind conjured what he'd been trying so hard to forget: two dead boys lying together on the ground—broken, lifeless, and undeniable.

"Why didn't you tell me before?" Ted asked, turning to face Martin.

"I didn't think you'd believe me if I just told you. I wasn't trying to trick you or anything. I'm sorry if it seems that way." Martin spoke carefully. "I don't know why, but you got stuck. I've been waiting for you to remember what happened, or come to terms with it, but I got tired of waiting. I hoped coming here would help you accept it."

Grieving the life he would never get to live, and thinking about how much he was going to miss his mom and dad, Ted sat down, put his head between his knees, and began to cry.

"Ted, I know how you feel, but everything's gonna be okay. Whatever happens next, whatever happens after this... I feel good about it for some reason."

"How can you feel good about any of this? It's not fair. We're dead. We're just kids and we're dead."

"Yeah, I guess it's not fair, but why would we stay here? I mean, do you really want to spend another night crying in your bed?"

Ted thought back to the last few nights; they had been the worst of his life. He wondered why he had made it so hard on himself, and for some reason the whole situation suddenly seemed absurd.

He let go of his fear and anger and accepted his fate, knowing he couldn't go on existing in a state of torture-denial any longer.

"I guess not," Ted answered at last, and stood up.

"That's more like it," Martin smiled.

"Martin, I'm really sorry. It was my idea to come here the other day, and it's my fault we died."

"Don't worry about it."

As they looked at each other, a cloud moved in front of the moon and covered the rock in darkness.

"Thanks for waiting for me, buddy." Ted gently punched Martin on the arm.

"No problem. I could never leave my best friend behind."

Ted was glad to have a friend who cared about him so much. He and Martin had never hugged, but it seemed like a good time for it. They reached out and held each other. After a few seconds, they began to wrestle and laugh.

When the clouds broke and the moon shone down again, the boys were gone, and a powerful wind carried the last echoes of their laughter down and away through the trees.

Stetson Ray lives in East Tennessee and spends his time writing novels, short stories, and screenplays. His stories have received multiple awards and prizes, including the Sue Ellen Hudson Award for Excellence in Writing, the James Still Prize for Fiction, and the Jesse Stuart Prize for Young Adult Fiction.

WHEN MEMORIES COME ALIVE

SUSAN E. ROGERS

He placed a pot of marigolds on the ground in front of the white marble gravestone. *In memory of Joseph Lintel.* Big Joe Lintel, they called his dad. And he was still Little Joe, despite his age. His father was forty-four when he died, one year older than he would be on his birthday tomorrow. These annual visits were a ritual now, born from an obligation.

If it wasn't for him, his father wouldn't be in that grave, or at least wouldn't have been there so young.

He needed a smoke before he got in the car, so his wife wouldn't smell it, and fished a crumpled pack out of the glove box along with a matchbook. Only one left. His hands trembled and his fingers fumbled with the matches. The first one wouldn't light and he shook so hard the cigarette broke in half. With a growl, he ripped off the broken end and flung it to the ground, grinding it beneath his heel. The next match flared and he brought it to the torn end of the cigarette, only to burn his lip with the flame.

Joe thought about his father a lot lately. Every time he looked in the mirror, his dad looked back. The same cropped blond hair with a streak of gray, the same crystal blue eyes, the same wrinkles that framed his mouth. The only thing missing was the scar, the raw red line that sliced his father's face diagonally in half from the right side of his chin through the sunken hollow that used to be his left eye. Big Joe suffered through the pain of infections and surgeries for a year before his death. Every day of that year reminded him that his father's suffering was because of him.

The grave sat in the second row of the cemetery, and the car was parked nearby. Leaving was always the hardest part, like turning his back on his father. Joe walked a few steps backwards and gave a half-hearted wave before he spun on his heel and trudged to the car. He fumbled with the key fob and dropped it, banged his head on the mirror getting up. The door finally open, he fell into the seat and slammed it shut.

He wiped the sweat from the back of his neck with his handkerchief and reached over to turn the air conditioner up full blast. His whole body twisted in the seat and he grunted as he pulled a wad of dollar bills from his pocket. The roll was secured with a rubber band and he checked to make sure it was intact before placing it on the seat next to the deli bag of sandwiches and the package of new white socks.

He was ready. As he'd been every year since his father died. The possibility was never erased, just because he hadn't needed them the year before. With one last glance at the grave, he shifted into drive and rolled down the narrow lane through the gate onto Washington Street. His teeth smashed together when the car hit a pothole.

"Son of a ..." The pain throbbed deep into his gums.

It wasn't the best part of the city to drive through even in the middle of the day and this street was the worst. It used to be one of the better districts, with shops and restaurants lining the sidewalks and fashionable apartments above. Now, sunlight reflected off the jagged edges of broken glass in windows along the ground floor of the yellow sandstone facades. Most buildings were deserted except for rats and the occasional vagrant. Empty nip bottles and fast-food wrappers competed for space in the gutter. Few people were out on the sidewalks in the midday heat and decay.

He wouldn't be here either if it wasn't the anniversary of his father's death. The neighborhood had changed dramatically since that day twenty-nine years ago when they buried his father in St. Mary's Cemetery. He had watched it deteriorate, a little at a time, when he drove through each year to and from his father's grave.

The iron gates of the cemetery entrance still loomed in the rearview mirror. The traffic light was four blocks ahead and the signal was green. If he drove fast enough, he should be able to reach it before it turned red. He pressed down on the gas pedal. Seconds later, the car hit another hole and bounced into the air, crashing against the asphalt edge on the way back down. His head hit the ceiling and his reflexes slammed on the brakes. Good thing there were no other vehicles around. He eased over to the curb and threw the car in park to wait for his shaking to subside.

Five minutes later, his thumping heart calmed and the sweat dried from his palms, he shifted into gear and pulled back out into the street. The light was red up ahead. His breath released in one long wheeze. If he slowed down, it might be green by the time he got there.

The first intersection slid by. The next pothole was big enough to swallow a cow but he saw it in time and veered around it. When he looked up, a quick movement near the traffic light caught his attention. A flutter in the wind, the flick of a rag. He stared through the white-hot glare. There was nothing there.

That day, thirty years ago, the sun was laser bright, too. His dad drove their new Chevy Malibu, white with red leather interior, down this very street, on the way to get his birthday present. He had begged and his father finally gave in—a new Powell-Peralta skateboard. Nothing but the best for Big Joe's kid. The shop was on this street, right after the traffic signal.

Two blocks ahead, the light turned green as he drove past the next intersection. Three teenage boys in t-shirts and jeans lounged on the sidewalk, hip-hop blaring from a wireless speaker on top of a busted newspaper vending machine. They yelled profanities as he drove by. He watched through the passenger's side mirror to make sure they didn't follow him, but they gave up and went back to their music. His gaze returned to the street ahead. A figure on the median startled him, a silhouette in the bright sunlight. Even with his eyes squeezed to a slit, he couldn't make out any features. But he could see the cardboard sign held up in the air.

That day, thirty years ago, the woman stood at that light in that same spot. A panhandler in tattered layers and wild hair who waved a cut-out piece of cardboard with NEED FOOD scrawled in smudged chalk. His father stopped when the light turned red and she staggered up to the car's open window. *Mister? Mister, please...* She stuck her hand through and his dad pushed her away. *Please, Mister...* His father spit in her face. *Get the hell away from me, you no-good lazy bitch!*

One block away now, about to pass through the last intersection. Agitated by the replay in his mind, he couldn't decide. Speed up. Slow down. The light taunted him. Maybe he could make it through. Not have to stop. *God, please.* Every year since that day, he had the same reaction as he approached the traffic signal. Every year, the same figure was there. Every year, the cardboard sign – YOU NEXT.

That day, thirty years ago, the woman wiped the spit from her face with her sleeve. The other hand sprang from her rags. The broken neck of a whiskey bottle slashed out. Blood spray-painted the car's interior. He could only stare at the cleaved flesh of his father's face, bone and muscle exposed, left eye dangling by a thread of tissue. A scream stuck in his throat as his father hyperventilated. He heard the cackle. Smelled the decay. He saw the toothless black gums when she growled at him. *Spittin' image, you next.* When the police got there, the woman was gone.

The light changed to yellow, then red. He glanced at the figure waiting up ahead. A woman with a dirty brown blanket over her shoulders that fluttered in the listless breeze, her frizzy hair tangled to a nest of greasy ropes, broken pink crocs below her mottled swollen ankles. Sunlight flashed in his eyes, reflected from the windshield of another car as it flew across the street in front of him. He blinked to clear his vision. When he could see again, the signal was green and the woman was gone. He looked left and then right. Vanished, except for the piece of cardboard on the ground. YOU NEXT. He rammed the gas pedal to the floor. The car bucked and skidded, then rocketed through the intersection.

A sigh of relief whooshed from his chest as he left the light behind. He unlocked his white-knuckled hands from the steering wheel one at a time and shook them out to release the tension. It was over for another year. He'd made it. His gaze rose to the rearview mirror with the intention of saying good riddance to that intersection and its memory. A flicker of shadow in the corner of his eye disappeared before he could see what it was. The light playing tricks, he thought as he forced a chuckle. The median was empty as the signal behind him turned red.

That day, thirty years ago, the skateboard shop was ahead on the right where that busted out storefront was now. There was no birthday present that year, all attention focused on saving his father's life. There was none the next year either, the funeral taking precedence. No, his birthdays were never a cause for celebration after that day, thirty years ago.

Another mile and he'd be at the entrance ramp to the highway, away from this street and its gut-wrenching recollections. A few deep breaths helped him relax. He turned on the radio to a classic rock station and started to sing along with the Rolling Stones' "Satisfaction." His fingers drummed the rhythm on the wheel. There was nothing to worry about. Maybe he'd take his wife out to dinner tonight to celebrate at that Italian place she liked.

His foot jammed down on the brake pedal. The tires squealed and the car fishtailed to a stop. A horn blared and the driver sped around him with a gesture. He didn't retain any of it. The face in the rearview paralyzed him.

The woman stared at him from the back seat, the one who was at the light a few minutes ago, and thirty years ago. She smirked through empty gums.

He tried to turn around but his body wouldn't cooperate. Instead, he closed his eyes, took a deep breath, and threw the shifter into park. Shoulders hunched, he twisted to confront the woman in the back seat.

Empty.

She wasn't on the floor either.

He turned back and slumped forward until his forehead rested on the steering wheel. Another horn honked, but he didn't look up.

Pressure closed in on his chest and his heartbeats double-plunked against his rib cage. He squeezed his eyes shut. "Aspirin," he whispered. "That's what they say—take aspirin if you're having a heart attack."

He avoided a glance at the back seat and opened the glove box. The mini first aid kit was right in front and the small white envelope marked "ASA" was on top. He tore it open and dumped the four pills onto his tongue. His mouth was too dry to swallow so he leaned back against the seat and chewed them to a bitter paste.

A knock next to his head made him jump. A police officer peeked in at him and motioned for him to roll down the window.

"Sir, are you all right?" the officer asked.

"Yes, I think so." His hands were clammy but the pressure was almost gone. "I was having chest pain, but it's better now."

"Do you want an ambulance?"

"No, no, no. I'm all right."

The officer left once she was convinced he was good to drive. He checked the back seat one more time and, reassured the woman wasn't there, put the car in drive. It was less than half a mile now to the highway and he could see the sign up ahead. This section of the street was even more desolate than near the cemetery. Rusted chain-link fence barricaded vacant lots from the sidewalk on the left. Decrepit buildings caved in on themselves on the right, broken glass and bricks spewed in all directions. Trash and debris clogged the gutters. The twisted skeleton of a burnt-out pickup blocked half of the lane in front of him. He shuddered.

A figure flashed in the passenger's side mirror. His head swiveled to the right. Nothing but empty street looked back. He returned his gaze to the highway ahead and clenched his teeth. Just a shadow. The ramp wasn't much farther ahead. Once he got there, he'd be safe. He'd be fine. Another dark flicker across the rearview. It was nothing, he told himself. He was being ridiculous.

A smell of putrid flesh permeated the air inside the car. He gagged and slapped his palm across his mouth and nose. A faint snicker from the back seat crescendoed to a mad cackle that echoed off the window glass. Bony fingers dug into his shoulder. He pulled the car over to the curb and shifted into park. His wide eyes looked up at her face in the rearview mirror. She threw her head back and laughed in a shrill squawk.

"What do you want?" His bottom lip quivered and his voice stuck in the back of his throat. The words came out a whispered croak.

"You!" Her shriek pierced his ears.

"You already killed my father."

"Ah, but he deserved it, didn't he, boy?" She cackled again and the noise screeched down his spine.

"I'll give you anything you need." He whimpered and tossed the bag of sandwiches at her. "Here. All for you." He held up the roll of ones. "I've got two hundred in cash. I can get you more."

"Too late for that." She batted the money aside. Her blackened finger pointed to the right. "That doorway was my crypt—starved to death, I did. Money's no help to me now."

The sunlight glinted off the sharp jagged edges of the whiskey bottle's broken neck as it slashed through the air. He squeezed his eyes shut, waiting for the pain, his muscles tensed, his body quaking.

Seconds passed. He felt nothing, heard nothing. Both eyes eased open to bright rainbows reflected from the prism of the car windows. He was alone. His breath exploded from his chest and tears gushed down his cheeks. Just a hallucination, that's all it was. This pilgrimage every year was getting too much for him. His father was gone and there was nothing he could do about it. Maybe it was time to forgive himself.

He swiped the dampness from his face, blew his nose on a tissue from the crushed box on the floor, and took a deep breath before he turned around to look in the back seat. He had to check, just in case. Empty. A half-smile played across his mouth. His eyes rolled heavenward and he whispered, "Thank you."

With a sigh, he shifted into drive, flipped on the turn signal, and checked the rearview for traffic. The car eased back into the street and he stared at the highway ramp straight ahead.

"Almost there. Gonna make it."

He glanced to his right at the piles of road salt and sand the city stored beneath the overpass. Battered chain link fencing ran around the perimeter, more broken than intact, twisted strings of metal that poked jagged fingers into the air around it. No, he wouldn't miss this annual trip one bit.

He directed his eyes back to the street in front of him and gasped. The old woman stood in the street between him and the highway ramp. He jerked the wheel hard to the right. The car spun twice, bounced off a cement barrier, and catapulted toward the fence.

He saw the metal pipe protruding from the chain link, as the car barreled straight toward it. Starbursts glistened off shards of glass as the pipe smashed through the windshield. His arms shot up to defend his head and he tried to duck. The pipe cut skin and muscle like a hot knife through butter and slit deep to the bone from chin to scalp, his left eye hanging by cords of nerves and veins. Blood splattered the seats and dash. A glint of light hit his right eye and he looked down at the broken neck of the whiskey bottle on the passenger's seat.

Through the haze, he heard a siren pierce the quiet of the street. His head lolled backward and his remaining eye gazed on the hag as she looked in through the broken windshield. Her squawking laugh grated against his raw nerves.

"You know, you look just like your father."

Susan E. Rogers lives in St. Pete Beach, Florida, transplanted from a Social Work career in Massachusetts. Moving was the catalyst to begin her life-long ambition to write. Her other interests include genealogy and psychic spirituality, and she often twists these into her writing. She has written and collaborated on numerous genealogical articles. She's released two books with independent publishers, with a third anticipated in Fall 2024. Since 2020, her short fiction appears in several anthologies, as well as a number of literary and genre magazines. Visit her author website at www.susanerogers.com and social media pages on Facebook and BlueSky.

VIOLENT ENDINGS

KATHERINE SILVA

It might have happened on this street: doused in rain as slick as oil, highlighted under a barrage of lights in all shades of neon. The chatter of passersby on the sidewalks yields to the roar of traffic, of the storm pounding the pavement, of the music coursing out of cars and clubs alike.

It might have happened here, you muse. But this place is nothing but transition. There's no permanency here, nothing to tether to or join. There's nothing familiar either and it solidifies your curiosity. You would know where it happened. After all, it was *the end*.

Endings aren't slaps with redness that fades quickly. They are mouths closing around you, teeth gnashing. They grind you up, break you down into the parts that totaled you. You lost the silly little things: the favorite colors you were drawn to as a baby, the memories of summers in childhood spent learning to cartwheel, the number of times tasting your own tears in the car where you were alone and didn't want others to see. Education, workforce, highs, lows, achievements, failures...

Those all vanished. And it became you; just you. A sum of human parts congealed in a mass of nothing drifting from place to place. Because death is never soft. The act of death is violence.

You may have floated into that blackness while lying in your bed. You may have let its tendrils wrap around you as you sat in a cozy chair and listened to a song you'd heard thousands of times over. Death might have snuck up on you when you were just waking to start a new day. But dying is never like lights fading, losing reception, static building...

Death is a thunder clap: bright, screaming, cataclysmic. It ripped you from a familiar world into this in-between one, poured you as liquid hot element into an amorphous thing and left you swimming in yourself. Nothing is up, nothing is down. No arms, no legs; all together in a flood of disorder and searing turbulence.

This is how you flow, if flow is the right way to put it. It's matter tumbling relentlessly, matter no one else can see or hear or feel. But even as the barest parts of you wage war with yourself, you move through the world that once was, examining each street, each building and each person.

The worst part is that thought and acuity are still with you. Being aware that you're no longer the thing you once were, the thing you spent decades shaping and molding and becoming left you a disjointed, quiet nothing for a while. Time and surround-ings were hard to perceive then through the mist of feeling, the ghost of emotion. Eventually, realization came back to you along with new apathy.

This street is not where it happened. You are certain now because you are passing it by, always onward toward *something*.

That something must be where the end happened. You'd decided this some time ago. You have spent so much time expe-riencing death that it has nearly eclipsed everything else about you. It would make sense that's what you hover toward: finality, where you passed from one phase to the next.

The lights dim and the haze overtakes the buildings as they darken. Concrete slabs strike up through the gray, evaporating into the sky. A single yellow rectangle alight in one; a red square in another. Endless towers bundled together like kindling in mid-smolder. Has your vision turned bloodshot or is it the darkness, stained by that one window?

You ease across the street toward that building, yanked by whatever force has summoned you across the world this whole time and a vestige of expectation creeps through you. This is it? This harrowing block of charcoal is the end. The red room is apotheosis.

Just as soon as you cross, you drift through the stone edifices and creep across a vacant lobby. The ceiling seems non-existent. There is no sound but if there were, you feel like it could echo on forever here.

This place is cold like the arctic. Where some businesses you've passed through hold pleasantness or some aspect of humanity, this one oozes austerity. Boredom. Decay. Each day the same again and again and again.

It's been some time since you've reacted to a place but you notice that every bit of your eddying self trembles here.

Elevators await you at the end of the room. For a moment, you remember the feeling of riding in one: your stomach dropping into your feet, the steady rumble beneath you. Something akin to expectation blips into your thoughts before you stream through the metal doors and just as quickly, pass through the back of the lift.

It's over. A lick of confusion gradually suffuses to indifference. You shudder through the backside of the building into volleys of rain and the misery of fog once more.

Not yet.

A sea of highways climbs up before you. Vehicles are locked in non-moving processions along the lanes, occupants leaning their tired heads against windows, some humming against pitch with their car stereos; all are stuck in limbo.

Limbo.

The word holds court in your thoughts as you glide through the cars. A never-ending desert of waiting, of expectation, of unexplained desire for something beyond this, whatever *this* is. This is what you're stuck in now, you decide. It only makes sense.

Making sense feels cathartic and despite your belief that you no longer feel, this catharsis sits in your thoughts like a warm electrical current. It's allowed as long as there is eventually progression even if time moves in circles, creating rings in your thoughts like those in a tree.

The highway stretches for what seems like eons; eventually becomes a bridge stretching over a wide and churning river. The people almost don't move anymore as you watch them. Maybe time has swallowed this pocket of the world. Perhaps they are in line waiting for the violence of death to strike them too.

The end of the bridge comes bringing with it a bend in the road that the cars follow while you careen into the forest they've avoided.

You leave the fog behind. The trees are too thick for it to pervade and what light you had before is snuffed into a warm, strange quiet: the kind like when you used to pull the blankets up over your head to protect you from the monsters you knew were lurking in your closet. The kind like when you found yourself in a room alone, bathed in sunlight, but felt the itch of eyes on you.

You wish you could drift faster here. Though you can not be seen, cannot be heard, cannot be felt, you know there is something here that knows you exist. There is something skulking among the trees examining your state of being with laughter poised on its tongue. And it takes shapes in your thoughts: first serpentine, then canine, then horrific... Too many arms, too many eyes, tendrils of muscle that cling like rope to the branches and whatever it can get hold of. Then, nothing at all.

It's you. The thing in the trees is you.

You're the monster waiting in the closet. The all-seeing eye glimpsing yourself in that sun-warmed room long ago.

You.

And while this new pain scrabbles through you, the woods go on and on. Memory is as sharp as thought and it's stuck in your nothing like a pin.

You'd told them so many times the monster was there. They'd never believed you. They'd told you to take medication. They'd told you to talk to a therapist. They'd told you to see, just see. Don't try to glance beyond a veil because there is none. You're making it up. It's all an overactive imagination. Too much coffee. Not enough sleep. Too much stress.

You must be wrong, they'd said, because we can't see it.

You've stopped paying much attention. Feeling has erupted like a boil brought to a head, leaking into every crevice, every crack of you, into the nothing...

It takes you time before you adjust to the pain. It takes time before you know that you were not wrong. You sensed this, all of this before it came but understood none of it because how could you? You and death weren't threaded together yet.

Awareness reprises in you. The woods are thinning toward a neighborhood: small homes in pastel colors, each one like the rest with little variations here and there. Lawn ornaments here, a hedge there, a rusted bicycle with flowers in the front basket...

It's quaint and calm and fills you. You're not sure with what. But your nothing suddenly has company and it's a feeling akin to being drugged. Clouds roiling up through you, blotting out the memories, clogging the pain and the perception both. It's pretty here. Pretty and possibly empty.

Even as the suspicion of this place festers within, you think of a bright pink journal set on a table in front of you. Pink is fun. Pink is symbolic. Festive, beautiful, feminine, alive, strong... Pink is a reminder to thrive. Pink is a small pill tucked in a little box with each letter of the week emblazoned on its lid. Pink is a hand gripped while crying. Pink is a presence; a *something*.

House after house coasts by and pink fades: pink like love, pink like promise, pink like dependence, pink like relying on other people...

And as the yards get larger and the roads longer, the violence of death unleashes a new anguish, one that scrapes at your already raw edges, pulls at your frays and ragged tears. Everything in motion and turbulent and pink gone: a new void left in its wake.

The grass lengthens and the hills swell and seem to breathe. Wind punches down through you and inflates your nothing. Yes, there is nothing. But you can still breathe somehow even through the pain.

The earth crumbles to sand. A commotion rages beyond its knolls and scurries up along the breath of air to greet you. You have no control of your speed, you never have. But it almost seems like this wind is sailing you toward that sound, filling a sail within.

An ocean awaits against a long and empty shore. Waves break into rocks and sand and the noise is calamitous and severe and beautiful. It's violence borne of consequence: the pull of the moon summoning and banishing the water to its whim.

It has no choice almost like you had none. Bidden to do whatever the powers that be wanted. As you swirl and collapse and crash against yourself, so does the water.

You have stopped. You hadn't realized it but how hovering over the water, observing its every lapse and burst, your nothing swells in synchronicity, longs for communion. Ferocity abates back into the sea before gathering in strength to dash back in again, to manifest greater and plunge down.

Pain is fading.

With each in and out, with each stir of wind that helps, this natural power takes your nothing. It splashes into your hollows and pulls more and more of you out with it with each lure of a wave.

You are consumed. More than consumed, you are transformed. Because while the ocean takes bit by bit, you join its magnificence. Its supremacy rushes through you like blood through arteries once did, expands in you like air used to in your lungs, and cries.

Yes.

It cries up from deep within: a scream wild enough to echo into the hills, batter against the grass, and reverberate in the sand. Delicate enough to turn to a whisper as it's dragged back from shore to culminate again.

The end. The end is here.

No, you realize. Not the end.

This is the beginning and you have arrived.

Katherine Silva is an ace Maine horror author, a connoisseur of coffee, and victim of cat shenanigans. Her favorite flavors of the genre mix grief and existentialism which she combines with her love of the New England wilderness in her works. She is a three-time Maine Literary Award finalist for speculative fiction and a member of the Horror Writers of Maine, The Horror Writers Association, and New England Horror Writers Association. Katherine is also editor-in-chief of Strange Wilds Press and an editor with Third Estate Books.

MARIGOLDS

JOSEPH STOUT

"It doesn't look like a serial killer's house."

"They never do. That's why they're so hard to catch." Sergeant Rebecca Vasquez checked the numbers on the house against her sticky note. 116 LeBlanc Dr. This was the place, an older Victorian home near the edge of town.

Three miles away, a landscaper named Jorge Villanueva was in a holding cell, arrested when a deputy caught him loading an unconscious eight-year-old into the back of his truck. That deputy had been in the right place at the right time, Vasquez thought. "You want the front or the back?"

Leon Gupton thought for a second. "I'll take the back."

She nodded. "Remember, kid, we aren't here to investigate. Our job is to keep the house secure until the search warrant comes in and forensics gets done with the truck." Eight girls, all under the age of eleven, had gone missing over the last three years. The case had escalated from their department to the State Police, then the FBI, and now they'd finally got their man. This killer was not getting off on a technicality.

"Sarge, I may be a rookie, but I know basic procedure." He got out and walked through an ornate gate. The house was surrounded by a black iron fence that would have looked more at home in an old cemetery than on a residential street.

Damn kid, Vasquez thought, taking a sip of her coffee. She hadn't wanted to be partnered with him, but the chief had insisted. Finding people who wanted to work on small-town police forces was hard, and he'd been willing to take the job. Of course, he could barely find his ticket book, but the chief didn't care about that as long as Vasquez could babysit him.

She took another sip of her coffee and reclined her seat. It would be a couple of hours before forensics got there, and she might as well be comfortable. It was going to be a late night, but she didn't mind. Halloween was coming, and her kids always wanted expensive costumes.

Gupton sat in a metal chair in the backyard. He could tell Villanueva loved his job. The flower beds and bushes were exquisite. In the center bed was a model of a Mayan pyramid, and other beds were decorated with gnomes and other ornaments.

By the garage, a row of marigolds had been planted. They'd always been his mother's favorite, and it made him happy to see them there. Above them, a basketball hoop had been mounted sideways on the garage wall.

Wait.

He walked over and counted. Eight desert marigold plants covered recently dug earth. Each one was smaller than the last, suggesting they'd been planted at different times. There was a fresh hole at the end of the line, but it was too big, too deep for a plant.

He was reaching for his radio when he heard the scream.

It came from inside the house. He raced across the yard and leaped onto the back porch. The windows on the door were covered, preventing him from seeing inside.

Another scream. He grabbed his radio. "Vasquez, you there?"

No answer.

He tried the door and it swung open. "Hello?"

"Help me!" It was a girl's voice. What if Jorge already had another victim here? He should go get Vasquez, but what if the victim couldn't wait that long? He pulled out his pistol and stepped through the door.

The covered windows and setting sun made the house dark. He turned on his flashlight and looked around. As beautiful as the outside had been, the inside was sparse. A table with a single chair was in one corner of the kitchen, a hot plate and coffee maker on the counter.

"I'm up here! Quick! It hurts!" On the far wall, a narrow staircase led upward, and he followed it to the second floor. The rooms were laid out around the center staircase, and he moved through them one at a time. They were all empty except for one, the back room overlooking the garage. It had a small cot, an armchair, and a chest of drawers. But there was no sign of whoever had been yelling. He looked for an entrance to the attic, but didn't see a trapdoor. Sighing, he decided to check the ground floor.

Vasquez saw the light through the front windows.

"Gupton, you there?" she radioed.

No answer.

She sighed and climbed out of the cruiser. Her back was sore, and she lifted her arms over her head to stretch before going through the gate. At the back of the house, she found the door swinging open.

"Fuck." She took out her sidearm and went inside. "Gupton!" she yelled, pulling out her own flashlight.

At the front of the house, someone screamed. She moved through the dining room toward the front hall. "Gupton! It's Vasquez! Don't shoot me!"

Gupton was halfway down the front stairs when something came out of the dining room. It looked like a woman, with a gun in her hands.

"Drop it!" he yelled.

She turned, and her mouth peeled back, pulling the skin that had covered her face to her neck, leaving only muscle, bone, and an evil smile. "Xibalba will rise," it hissed.

He fired as fast as he could.

Vasquez saw the first flash, then heard the shot. Without thinking, she turned and opened fire. She felt the impact of the rounds hitting her, driving her to the floor. As she fell, her gun hit the ground and slid out of reach.

Two rounds hit Gupton, both in the vest, and the impact made him take a step back, still firing. He lost his footing and fell down the stairs. Groaning from the pain, he tried to push himself up, but his left arm didn't want to work. Using his right, he got to his feet. He waved the flashlight along the floor, looking for the body of the thing he had shot.

"Shit! Sergeant!" She was bleeding from her neck, just above her bulletproof vest. The thing he saw must have shot her. Where had it gone? He turned his head, looking into the dark rooms around him, but he saw nothing.

"Gupton," Vasquez breathed. "He was just here, the gunman."

"Relax, Sarge," he knelt next to her. The bullet must have hit a blood vessel. He pressed on the wound as he reached for his radio. "10-999, 10-999, officer down, LeBlanc Drive. Do you copy?"

Nothing.

The blood was still flowing out. He pulled the radio off his belt and confirmed the power light was on. "Ten-Nine-Nine-Nine, officer has been shot, LeBlanc Drive." He let go of the transmit button and got nothing but silence. The front door was a few feet away, and the squad car beyond it, but that meant leaving the Sergeant alone.

He felt around behind him for his gun, but found a foot instead. Gupton turned slowly.

It was a little girl, perhaps nine years old, with long blonde hair wearing a purple dress.

"Hey there, can you help me?" Gupton asked

"Gupton!" He grabbed the Sergeant's hand. She was fading. He considered trying to find the artery, but he didn't want to take pressure off the wound.

"You helped us," another voice said. A red-haired girl was standing by the front door, holding the sergeant's gun.

"You brought the sacrifice," a third girl, a freckled brunette, said. She stood at the sergeant's head, holding a marigold. Gupton realized who they were.

He grabbed his radio. "Base, this is Gupton, is anyone there?"

"It won't work," the redhead said. "Master made sure of that."

Vasquez groaned, then exhaled, closing her eyes.

"No!" Gupton put his ear to her mouth, but she wasn't breathing. He pushed down on her chest, and a shot of blood spurted from her neck.

"CPR won't help," the brunette said. "She lost too much blood."

Gupton shook his head. "She can't be dead." The sergeant's eyes were open, staring at him.

"But she is," the blonde said. "Don't worry. We needed her like this."

"We?"

Five more girls appeared, surrounding them.

"We are going to take you to Master," the brunette said.

"Carry her," the redhead ordered.

"What if I say no?"

She pointed the gun at him. "You die. Then we take control of your body."

"But my arm?"

The blonde touched him and the pain in his arm vanished.

"What the hell?"

"Let's go." The redhead studied the shadowy darkness. "Master will rise soon."

He lifted Vasquez, cradling her in his arms, feeling the sticky blood soaking into his uniform.

"Follow me," the blonde said. She opened a door under the stairs and led them into the basement.

The passage had been dug out from the side of the basement. It opened up after twenty feet, into a dirt-walled room with a large stone in the center. Spots on the stone were darker than the rock, and Gupton realized it was blood.

"Put her there," the blonde commanded, and Gupton laid Vasquez on the stone.

A metal door behind the stone began to glow.

"The master awakens," the brunette said.

"The master?" Gupton asked.

"He is the one who freed us from our mortal bonds," the blonde said.

"We are to serve him for all eternity," said the brunette.

"It is an honor higher than any other," the redhead finished.

The door swung open. A hand emerged first, its skin deep black with gold and silver tattoos. As it opened wider, the man stepped forward, barely able to pass under the top of the door. He was nude except for a cloth at his loin, and the tattoos covered his body.

"Master!" they called.

"Girls." He knelt, and they took turns embracing him. Then he stood and looked at the body on the stone. "Her spirit was captured?"

The redhead nodded. "Just like you showed us."

He waved a hand over the rock, and it began to glow. "Excellent." He sat next to Vasquez and reached for her head.

"Don't touch her!" Gupton lunged at the tattooed man, but found himself frozen in place.

"You are her partner?" he asked, running his fingers through her hair. "Don't worry, you will have a job too."

"A job?"

The brunette spoke up. "Like us, you will serve him for all eternity."

"Serve him? I don't even know who he is."

"I am a God of Death, a being with a power you will never understand. The ancient Maya called me Vucub Came, Seven Death. With Hun Came, I ruled over Xibalba, the Underworld. Unfortunately, we were defeated by ones called the Hero Twins, and vanquished from Xibalba. Now, I intend to resurrect Xibalba in all its glory, without the foolishness of Hun Came to bring us down."

"And you think you can do this by killing kids and cops?"

"The choice of victims is insignificant, so long as there are nine of them. Nine is a deep part of the magic of Xibalba. There are nine gods of Xibalba: myself, Hun Came, and the seven lesser gods. Xibalba also has nine levels. When I resurrect it, each of the captured souls will rule over one of the levels. I will be elevated from one of many to the supreme God of Death, ruler of Xibalba."

The rock glowed brighter, and he smiled. "It is time, girls. Seal the house."

The girls linked hands in a circle around the altar, and a green light formed in the center, then exploded past the walls of the chamber. "We are ready, master," the redhead said.

"Good. Good." He turned to Gupton and gestured to Vasquez. "Did you know you killed her?"

"I didn't kill Vasquez."

"But you did. You see, once you pass the gate, we control your perception of your senses. It was easy for Abigail to block you from hearing each other's calls, and make her appear to be a monster."

The redhead grinned at the God's praise. "You shot her. I saw you."

"That's impossible!"

"It's the truth, and it's something you'll have to live with for all eternity," she said.

"No!" He fell to the ground, and tears rolled down his face. Vucub Came put a hand on his shoulder.

"You did good work for us. Now the time has come to restore Xibalba!"

"I'll stop you," Gupton said, wishing he was convinced.

"No, you won't. Your policemen tried, but they failed. They arrested the Villanueva slave and the girl who was supposed to be the last sacrifice. Fortunately, I am adaptable. This woman will become the ninth sacrifice, and you will take Villanueva's place. When her body is consumed and Vasquez takes her eternal form, the ancient magic will pull our souls from the earth. But someone must be left behind to remember us, or the magic will be incomplete," he smiled at Gupton. "That's where you come in."

The girls surrounded him, then the redhead grabbed him and dragged him to a stake behind the rock. She tied his hands to it, as the blonde hung a wreath of marigolds around his neck.

"Wait, what about their parents, Vasquez's children, won't they remember?"

The God shook his head. "When their souls are pulled to Xibalba, it will be as if they didn't exist. Their entire lives will be stored here, their possessions, their memories, everything that tied them to this world. Even their bones will remain here, in the graves you saw earlier. And you. You will remember what the world forgets and bear the horror of it for all eternity!"

A clock sounded somewhere upstairs. "The Dark Hour of Nine has come!" The girls and Villanueva joined hands in a circle, surrounding Gupton. Abigail looked at Gupton and smiled. "Sorry to leave you like this. We'll take good care of her."

The ninth chime sounded as he tried to pull away, and the room was consumed by fire, then darkness.

A rusty car sits in the backyard of 116 LeBlanc Drive, shielded from view by a tall iron fence. It may have been a police car, but it's hard to tell now, overgrown with vines.

No one has lived here for years, but the house never seems to age. It just sinks deeper into the jungle growing around it.

Inside, the possessions of ten people fill the rooms. Jump ropes, dolls, two police badges, gardening equipment, clothes, sonograms, everything that might mark a person's existence.

In one room, nine lives are condensed to tall stacks of leather-bound volumes.

The tenth soul remains, trapped behind the iron gate forever. Gupton can wander as far as the gate, the barrier to the world he remembers, the world without the nine souls whose possessions fill this house.

But he doesn't.

He sits on the bed in the back room, next to the only window that isn't covered. From it, he can see the garage wall, with nine marigold plants growing feral. He's read the books, studied the souls claimed by Vucub Came to rule over Xibalba. Eight girls and a woman, stolen from this world to help rule over another.

Even without the marigolds, he would remember.

How could he forget?

D.L. Winchester lives in the foothills of southern Appalachia. A former mortician, his work searches the darkness to find tales worth telling. He is the author of over three hundred obituaries, numerous short stories, and the upcoming Flash Fiction Collection "A Terrible Place." In his spare time, he can be found searching for inspiration in the world around him and trying to keep his children from becoming the next generation of horror villains.

Also From Undertaker Books

Ink Vine

Elizabeth Broadbent

Shadows of Appalachia

D.L. Winchester

The Taste of Women

Cyan LeBlanc

Mastering The Art of Female Cookery

Cyan LeBlanc

In Memory of Exoskeltons

Rebecca Cuthbert

Stories To Take To Your Grave: Vol. 1(Anthology)

A Terrible Place and Other Flashes of Darkness

D.L. Winchester

The Triangle + The Deep Double Feature

Robert P. Ottone

Silent Mine

C.M. Saunders

Odd Jobs: Six Files from the Department of Inhuman Resources(Anthology)

Judicial Homicide (Anthology)

Bodily Harm
Deborah Sheldon

The Screaming House
D.L. Winchester

Wilder Creatures
Nadia Steven Rysing

Ninety-Eight Sabers
Elizabeth Broadbent

SELF-MADE MONSTERS
Rebecca Cuthbert

If you are a fan of horror stories and tales,
you'll want to follow Undertaker Books.

We're bringing you stories to take to your grave.
SIGN UP FOR OUR NEWSLETTER ONLINE